CUT
FROM
FIRE

JOSHUA RAVEN

Red Ink. Publishing

First published in the UK by Blue Fish Publishing Limited in 2013. This edition published in the UK by Red Ink Publishing Limited, 2025.

© 2025 Red Ink Publishing Limited www.5fingers.co.uk

All rights reserved.

5fingers is a trademark of Red Ink Publishing Limited

This novel is a work of fiction. Names and characters are the product of the author's imagination and any resemblance to actual persons, living or dead, is entirely coincidental.

Arif A Mohamed has asserted his rights under the Copyright, Designs and Patents Act, 1988 to be identified as the author of this work.

The moral right of the author has been asserted

A catalogue record for this book is available from the British Library

Cover Design by JD Smith.

Title Production by The BookWhisperer

ISBN(eBook): 978-1-0685674-6-9
ISBN(Paperback): 978-1-0685674-7-6
ISBN(Hardcover): 978-1-0685674-8-3

This book is dedicated to my three children, R, J & C. You are so awesome, and I love you dearly and unconditionally.

Tommy Thumb, Tommy Thumb Where are you?
Here I am, here I am How do you do?

12345

CHAPTER I

Two bolts of lightning slashed through the magenta clouds, one a blinding white, the other a sharp, chrysolite-green. They struck the earth in a crackling burst, twisting and shaping into two men astride pale stallions, their hooves planted solidly in the churned soil. Above, the heavy clouds hung low, casting an ominous veil over the scene.

"The enemy has snatched the higher ground today," noted one of the two. He sat upright, his broad shoulders swaying as the horse undulated gently. Dressed in a white tunic and a light metal breastplate, the handle of his sword was easily accessible.

The other man was also muscular, with long white hair and an intense but handsome face. On his head sat a thin crown, simple in design, little more than a circle of platinum that denoted his royalty.

As he gazed at the hilltops, his eyes shone like the sun. His horse sniffed the air and waited.

At last, he spoke. "Come, Sandalphon. It's time to fight."

RACHEL STUMBLED ALONG A STRANGE ROAD, staring wildly around her. The swirling, violet, apocalyptic sky from her dreams hung above her. A bloodthirsty wind tore at her clothes, making her shiver. Trees and rocks seemed to hang in the air, but her hand moved through empty space when she tried to touch them.

At the edges of her peripheral vision, she could see massive superstructures. But these disappeared when she turned her head to look at them. Even the narrow path she walked on seemed insubstantial, with gaping holes leading down into an abyss. The top of an ice-capped mountain made of dark red rock appeared above her head. A blood-red moon presided over it all.

Confused and lonely, she walked a few paces, hugging her arms around her body. She jumped at an unfamiliar noise behind her but, spinning around, saw nothing.

The alien road stretched far ahead. It wound around a set of boulders the colour of dried blood, which overlaid a forest of fiery trees, like a double-exposure photograph that displayed the impossible. She decided to follow the long, narrow road that wound through this otherworldly valley. After all, the only way was forward now.

Rachel had left the stone head far behind her. It was identical to the one she had passed through on Griffton Cliff at the entrance to this world, but unlike the first doorway, this one seemed inert. It emitted no buzz of electricity, and there was no apparent way to enter it. She was stuck here now, with no way back.

IT WASN'T long before the fear came. This was no ordinary fear, like the hopeless anxiety of being chased by a panther. Nor was it the fretfulness you get from being lost, but a heavy presence that fell on her and dragged her down. It was a pressure on her head, a weight on her emotions, pulling her earthwards to an early grave.

She trudged through a valley circled by panoramic mountains, afraid of the purple sky and the floating rocks, watchful for a pursuer and nervous about the path she trod.

Apart from the fear, she felt little else, which was strange. There was no hunger or thirst, no urge to go to the toilet. There were no odours here that she could detect. Although she shivered, she did not feel cold. The ground was responsive underfoot, not hard, not soft. It was like she was walking through a dream, scared and alone.

The massive valley stretched out before her, edged with creeks and gullies that clung to the mountain foothills. She realised the blood-red moon was more likely a sun, muted and discoloured by the thick atmosphere hanging over the land. The edge of the orb was bright, just like the sun back home. The difference was that there was no heat from this one—or at least none she could feel.

"Are you ill, Rach?" she whispered to herself. "Maybe I'm sick," she said aloud.

Through the dread, Rachel clung to a faint hope that she would see Daniel, Arabella, Micah, and the children again. Perhaps they had sprinted through the gateway and made better progress through the valley? If she carried on walking, surely she would find them? Why hadn't they waited for her, though? They must have known she would follow them once they entered the doorway.

But no, they hadn't waited for her. It was the same old story; no one waited for her. Friends deserted her, family abandoned her, and she was always left on her own.

First, it was her mother, the bedrock of her life, who had left this world when she was just nine years old. Then, her father had abandoned her emotionally, withdrawing into himself and becoming little more than a shell of a man. Her best friend of many years, Lara Summer—with whom she had built a mansion of memories spanning their entire school career—had left, too. She was living it up in sunny California and hadn't even bothered to get in touch. And then there was her boyfriend, Lake. It felt like he'd abandoned her as well. He might have shown more loyalty—fancy going after that nasty little Kumi girl who'd just appeared on the scene!

But no, she was kidding herself. Rachel was the problem. She was the common denominator, the one thing that was consistent in all of these relationships and situations. The one thing that remained the same, whether it was about her mum, her dad, her friends, or Lake, was Rachel Race herself.

"It would be better if I was dead," she concluded.

The valley had risen gently, changing from a long plateau to a rocky ascent. She thought about how one would go about dying in this dream world. If you died here, would that mean you died in real life? Since she didn't feel the cold, does that mean she wouldn't feel pain? These were unknowns.

Like an automaton, she traversed the incline, gradually gaining a broader view of the basin. It was an oval valley shaped like one of her dad's Pyrex dishes. The stone head was now just a dot at the valley's edge, and beyond it, she couldn't see. The dark red mountains, capped with ice, blocked her view of the land beyond, but she could make out deep, shadowed crevasses and long fissures cutting down the mountainsides and plunging into the ground.

She didn't feel ready to think about the Dream Fighters, who had leapt out of the imagination and into real life. She pushed away the memory of the conversation with the businessman, the one who channelled the spirit of that demon, Samyaza. She shivered at the memory.

DOWN BENEATH THE SURFACE, slow hands were at work. They were stitching and melding, picking and smoothing, and completing the Malkin. Its horrible eyes stared out from their deep sockets, lifelike and, at the same time, shockingly lifeless.

Arms stuck out at an unnatural forty-five degrees. The Malkin was propped up against a high table, covered in scraps of material, long hair, and bone fragments. In places, grotesque and unrecognisable objects were piled up. There were several pots of liquid, red, brown, and black, and a tray full of metal instruments.

"Carefully does it. There's no use rushing these things," said the gravelly voice. There was an icy chuckle.

"One finger, one thumb keep moving; one finger, one thumb keep moving; one finger, one thumb keep moving; we'll all be merry and bright," sang the man in a tuneless growl.

"And so, hi ho, hi ho, so packed full of secrets you are, riddled with riddles. You are everywhere and nowhere, baby. Easy does it." He coughed a painful and raking cough, sitting back to look at his handiwork. His round, red face glowed in the torchlight. He had a high forehead with receding grey hair, red eyes with arched eyebrows above, and a horrible grin below. Lips parted to reveal yellow teeth.

"Not bad. Not good but really not bad at all. You, my dear, are almost finished. Then you have work to do."

Somebody appeared at the top of the steps. It was a small albino boy with a pointed chin and round head devoid of hair. He had small black button eyes that stared forward and arms that were limp at his sides. He wore a dark T-shirt with long trousers over his pale feet.

"It's okay. You can come down."

Noiselessly, the small boy tripped into the room with light steps, his arms still motionless. He stared at the man all the while, and when he approached him, he stood by his side but remained silent. They both stared at the Malkin for some time before the craftsman spoke again.

"I see," he mumbled, though the boy hadn't spoken once. "In that case, we should go up and greet her. Don't you think?"

The boy stared unblinking with his weird black eyes. A lizard tongue slipped over his thin lips.

Somebody was following Rachel. She was absolutely sure of it. She had climbed a steep bank and was now on a narrow path that wound around a series of hills, with a valley below a sheer drop. There was no way of retracing her precarious steps. The only way was up.

"I do not want to be here," she muttered through gritted teeth. She glanced around at the apocalyptic sky, the strange sun, or moon, or whatever it was, and the shifting vale. Mammoth rocks still seemed to defy gravity, twisting slowly high above the ground.

It would be beautiful if it wasn't so shocking. Wild purples and reds filled the sky. Down in the mighty valley, trees crisscrossed, growing horizontally or vertically, straight out of each other. Crazy branches fanned out in all directions, forming an impenetrable forest. There was no sign of human life. The fear squeezed her heart again, its grip like fangs on a bony hand. She swallowed her panic and set her will to go on. Placing one foot in front of the other, she trod the craggy path, its sharp black and grey stones wedged into the dark earth. It led her to higher ground. At the next turn, the path levelled out suddenly and unexpectedly, stretching toward a broad plain on her right.

A pale boy waited in the middle distance. He looked about five or six years old, patient but forlorn. Far behind him was a dark house, squatting like a heavy toad at the centre of the plain. The mountain peaks towered all around them, sheer fingers of rock, soaring ever upwards towards the purple swirling canopy.

The boy stood stock-still and waited for her to approach.

CHAPTER 2

"Hello. Do you live here? Where are we?" asked Rachel.

The strange bubble-headed boy said nothing, so Rachel tried again.

"I mean, what is this place? I came through some sort of doorway: a stone head. Like the one down in the valley, you know?"

The boy stared at her through tiny black eyes that were impossible to read. His thin lips were clamped shut.

"Have you seen any other people? I lost my friends. They were with me, but now they're gone. There are two men, a woman, and two boys. Boys like you. Well, not exactly like you. Sorry, no offence." She was aware she was jabbering and made herself stop and take a deep breath. She was just pleased to find someone vaguely human to talk to.

They were on an even stone plateau the colour of coal, etched with deep marks. Snow-capped mountains faded in and out of her peripheral vision. She could feel the icy wind blowing through the massive open space but felt the chill this time. It flayed her skin, and she felt it whipping around her internal organs, freezing her to the bone.

He was a very strange boy for sure, thought Rachel. He was incredibly pale, an albino, with almost no hair and odd arms that didn't move. The fact that he didn't say anything was even more unusual, but then he could be mute. It was unnerving her, the way he looked at her without responding.

She tried again, "Okay, then, do you know how I can get home? The door isn't working. I mean, that stone thing. Is there a knack to it? How do you switch it on?"

The boy turned around and started walking away, back to the house.

"Hey," she called softly. "Can you help me?" The funny little boy was the most normal thing she had encountered in this strange land. So, she didn't want to let him go, even though she was scared of what would happen if she followed him. It never seemed to bode well for her, this sort of thing, she thought.

Before long, she scampered after him. After all, he was her only hope. He didn't seem that dangerous, just odd. The dark house loomed before her, wide and tumbledown. It was made of wood, with paint-faded window frames and a roof that looked like it was about to slide off. There was no garden, gate, or porch, just a big fat house that could have dropped out of the sky and landed on the rock. The people who lived there had a great view of the mountains, though.

"Is there someone I can talk to?" she asked desperately. Again, there was no answer.

RACHEL FOUND herself sitting on a wooden chair, wondering exactly how she had allowed herself to enter a strange man's house. He had introduced himself as Zaelaza but added, "Call me Zed." Rachel felt incredibly uncomfortable.

The man half laughed, half sneered, showing a ragged row of yellow teeth. He looked sunburnt or red-faced with drink, something she had often seen with her dad.

She wondered what her father, Eddie, was doing right now and if he had even noticed she was gone. If only he had been more of a dad to her. If only he had known how to protect her better.

"Don't be nervous, we are your friends. There's nothing to fear here. We don't get many visitors, and life is so banal. Or boring, as you youngsters say. Olm here will look after you, won't you, my boy? Meanwhile, let me fix you a drink. Tea? I'm sure you like tea. Everyone likes tea." The man had a deep and sarcastic voice, but Rachel nodded, even though she wasn't sure if she had any appetite for food or drink.

"Is he your son? Does he have any brothers or sisters? Not that it's a bad thing to be an only child. I mean, I am, and it isn't a problem," she said as he bustled about his tiny kitchen, which adjoined the dark front room.

She looked around her, less self-conscious now she was out of his microscopic gaze. He had a collection of functional furniture items, including a couple of chairs, a solid dining table, and a stubby bookcase. It was a bachelor's home, and she guessed there was no Mrs Zed.

A wide, dark fireplace sat at the base of one wall, with black marks covering the back. There were no pictures on the walls and no electronics. She had clearly stepped into the dark ages. She checked her phone discretely, which was in her jeans pocket. No network, no wireless: she was right. She hid it away again.

"He's my boy. He doesn't say much, but he's company for me," the man called from the kitchen.

Zed told her she was in what he called "the mezzanine," which was "neither here nor there." It was "not such a great place to live but better than some. Of course, some people call it the underworld, but in reality, it was really located between the worlds, which is why I refer to it as a mezzanine place".

He claimed he hadn't seen Micah or Daniel and his family but assured Rachel he'd keep an eye out. Rachel was dubious. As for getting home, he said he knew someone who could help with that but would have to contact them. Rachel couldn't see a telephone or a computer anywhere, so she wondered how he proposed to do that.

"What name do you go by, little missy?"

With a sudden rush of confidence, Rachel asserted her name was Maggie. Maggie McKenzie.

Zed backed out of the kitchen with a hot mug of tea in his hand. "Okay then. Here you go, Maggie McKenzie. Drink up, my little friend." He gave her a creepy grin.

He stood with the strange bald kid by his side, who stared back silently, unblinking, with his little paws clenched into fists at the ends of his straight arms.

They made an unusual pair. Zed was red-faced, unshaven, and slightly overweight with receding flyaway hair. He had bright blue eyes that were red-veined and penetrating. He was like the crazy uncle at a Christmas party. The alien boy was just an oddity, evidently on leave from the mothership. In her head, Rachel heard herself saying, "Okay, guys, enough. This is all too weird. I need to get out of here, and I need to get out of here now."

But instead, she hid her fear by smiling and sipping her tea.

"So, tell me, Maggie, what happened to your hand there? I hope you don't mind me asking, but I kind of specialise in that sort of thing. I'm also very curious by nature. Do tell me."

"Are you a surgeon?"

"Something like that, little miss."

Rachel bit her lip. She thought she felt the stump of her finger throb. "It was kind of like an industrial accident. I was working on a production line, and, you know, I got a bit too close to the machinery. It was a while ago. I don't really like to talk about it."

"Oh, I see," said Zed. He stared for a couple of moments at

her hand but quickly seemed to grow bored and move on. "Speaking of work, it's time that I got back to mine. I work downstairs, in the basement. Top secret stuff."

He nodded his head to the door over at the far wall. As Rachel looked over, a cold dread came over her.

Seeing her face, Zed said, "I have a job to do: a purpose. Do you? Do you have a purpose? What's your purpose, little miss?"

"Um. I don't really know," said Rachel flatly.

"I see. Well, anyway. Olm will look after you until I can reach my friend. Then we will get you home."

The kid seemed to stick his chest out a little more and plant his arms further back. Apart from that, his expression remained the same.

Zed opened the door, and Rachel felt a wave coming over her, a sense of hideous evil coming from whatever was on the other side of the door. Something deep inside her, her very spirit, fought to propel her out of the house, out of this mezzanine world, and far away from whatever was in the basement.

The feeling of evil was palpable. It was stronger than the presence she had felt in the dining room at the Griffton Metropolitan Hotel: the time she had sat opposite Samyaza in the businessman's body, Benson Steel. This was a feeling that threatened to engulf her in terror, leaving her wide-eyed and drooling. Whatever was down there didn't just want to destroy her. It wanted to eradicate anything good in this world. Rachel started to feel herself swoon.

Fear overwhelmed her as she realised. It was the tea. Zed had put something into the tea that was making her head and limbs feel heavy. Some sort of poison.

Her eyelids started to flutter. Before they closed, she saw a long black tongue, like a strip of felt, pass across the boy's thin lips. It happened in a split second, but she saw it clearly. Then she passed out.

"WHAT DID you guys do to me?" slurred Rachel. She wasn't confident that her words came out as anything other than a long string of vowels from the back of her throat.

The round-headed boy stood next to her. She was lying on a bed, fully clothed. Her brain swam inside her head, but she could see she was in a small room with a low ceiling. Apparently, patches of dark brown paint had been randomly applied to a light brown wall. The room was empty except for the bed. Through a small dark-wood window, she could see the purple sky.

She was trapped.

The boy, Olm, had something in his hand. With horror, she realised it was a dead creature. He raised it to her, and she saw him move either of his arms for the first time. Soft guts and blood oozed through his fingers and pooled on the wooden floor.

She heard Zed's voice saying, "My boy likes you. I see he's brought you a gift." Rachel's eyes rolled involuntarily in her head. If it was a gift, it was an utterly inappropriate one.

"Why are you keeping me here?"

"We're waiting, remember?" he said in reassuring tones.

Olm stood too close for comfort, arms rooted by his side, pinning her with his weird black eyes.

To her horror, Rachel realised there were now two identical kids standing side by side. She thought her eyes were deceiving her, but there were clearly two small boys. They were both albinos, with black defiant eyes that refused to blink and long, shabby trousers that fell over their bare feet.

"But I thought you only had one son," said Rachel.

"Oh, he does that sometimes. You see, he's a Spawner." Rachel stared at the three of them, lost for words.

"Come now, you must drink your tea before it gets cold," said Zed, feeding Rachel her drink. She was unable to stop him from pouring it down her throat.

Zed continued, "Cold tea is horrid. Olm here tried to give

me cold tea once and I had to discipline him. He didn't make that mistake twice. No, Miss Maggie must have her tea. It helps to pass the time. Time for tea, tea for two. Time passes, tick-tock. Time to work, time to sleep."

As Rachel slid into the blackness, she heard Zed singing in a deep, growling voice.

"Tommy Thumb, Tommy Thumb, where are you? Here I am, here I am, how do you do? Peter Pointer, Peter Pointer, where are you? Here I am, here I am, how do you do?"

Rachel's head swam with the ghosts of dreams and the swirling sound of a vortex gnawing at the edges of her sanity. She was slipping into a dream within a dream, in a land that didn't exist: a mezzanine world where no one would ever find her.

And still, her captor sang. "Toby Tall, Toby Tall, where are you? Here I am, here I am, how do you do? Ruby Ring, Ruby Ring, where are you? Here I am, here I am, how do you do?"

At the peak of her panic, amid the black mist, the rhythmic words rotated inside her head.

"Baby Small, Baby Small, where are you? Here I am, here I am, how do you do?" She didn't know whether she heard the end of the rhyme but was surely glad when she lost consciousness.

And all the while, Zed sang, "Fingers all, Fingers all, where are you? Here we are, here we are, how do you do?"

CHAPTER 3

Eddie Race sat up in bed. He was a hulking mountain of a man with curly clumps of dark brown hair and semi-circles under his eyes that resembled the marks from a coffee mug. He was unshaven, unfit, and badly in need of a wash.

His room was a tip. In just two days, plates and papers, mugs, clothes, and cutlery had managed to get everywhere. It was late morning on a Sunday, and the curtains were closed. The radio burbled, too quiet to pick up words but loud enough to provide Eddie company. Downstairs, at the foot of the front door, yesterday's post sat unopened.

Since Rachel had disappeared, he'd felt wretched. For months, he knew, he had failed to connect with her in any meaningful way. When she had the car accident, he wasn't there for her. He couldn't even bring himself to ask her about it afterwards. He was a disgrace to himself, a terrible father, and a huge let-down for her.

And so, he did what he always did. He ignored it and buried himself in his work, carpentry jobs, and the steady stream of plumbing emergencies. Only, the last few days, he felt he was losing his mind, and work held little interest for him anymore.

He knew he'd completely betrayed Rachel by doing his master's bidding last week and allowing the fake uncle to lead her into danger. What sort of father would do that? She was a seventeen-year-old girl, for crying out loud: his own flesh and blood. He even kept up the charade when she returned, sweeping the incident away.

He never found out what had happened, and she didn't speak of it. He just hoped she'd been able to look after herself in the face of that monster, Samyaza. From her silence, he sensed something bad had happened. She was almost as good at hiding things as he was.

Then, two days ago, on Friday, she went missing. He thought about calling her work. It was either the record shop or the other place. He considered calling her friends, maybe the lad in the newspaper with the funny name or the hippy girl with the name of a Scottish island. Beyond them, he didn't really know who her friends were anymore.

He even thought about telling the police but quickly abandoned the idea, fearing they would arrest him for her murder. She'd probably just done a runner to a friend's house. It wouldn't be the first time, and he wouldn't blame her.

But still, it lay heavy on him. He was the reason she had gone. Now, he'd lost his wife and his daughter.

And so, he returned to his bed on Saturday morning when she hadn't returned home, getting up only when he needed food, drink, or the bathroom. The rest of the time, he lay in a sleepless fog, staring into space, watching his fears spiral around him.

As he lay there, a string of words began to form in his head. It was as though his name was being sounded. Except it was his full name, not the shortened version everyone used. The last time he'd heard his full name spoken was when it had tumbled from the lips of his wife, his darling Maryam, who used it every so often and always affectionately and with humour. This time, it wasn't her saying it because she was dead and gone.

"Edward Malcolm Joseph Race." He listened anxiously to the disembodied voice in his mind, trembling slightly.

"Please, not again," he said. He pushed his big hands against his eyes and gave them a rub. Pretty patterns swirled around his head, the intricate shapes you see when you press your palms into your eyes.

His name rang out again in his head. "Edward Malcolm Joseph Race. Get up, take a shower, and get dressed. I have work for you to do."

"I'm sick of your games, Samyaza," he roared. "Why don't you just leave me alone? Leave me alone," he trailed off. But the voice was gone, and he was left petitioning the walls of his empty room.

⤜ 12345 ⤛

RACHEL WOKE up from what felt like a long, dreamless sleep. It took time to focus her eyes, and when she finally did, she stifled a scream. She counted five or six of the little boys by her bed. They were identical, wearing anthracite-grey T-shirts and shabby trousers. One of the boys was still holding the dead creature in his hand.

Rachel screamed.

She saw the man, Zed, relaxing in a wooden chair by the far wall.

"What am I doing here?" slurred Rachel. Her tongue was a slimy slug with a mind of its own.

"Let me go. Please let me go."

"We're waiting, remember? Passing time, being patient, waiting until you can fly away home. If you're waiting for a rescue—from the Rescuer, perhaps—forget it. He's a liar. No, you can't trust him. He might promise the world, but when it comes to the crunch, he'll let you down. Everyone knows that when the chips are down, he's nowhere to be found." Rachel closed her eyes.

"He'll turn you into a robot. He'll make you his slave. No, you can't trust the Rescuer," Zed continued. "But you can trust me. You can count on me, one, two, three. I sent word to my master, and he's coming to you right away. He'll take you back safely to your world. For some reason, Maggie, he's taken a special interest in you. But when he comes, we won't know what he looks like. He takes many forms."

"Master?" Rachel managed. "You're talking about Samyaza?" Her head was clearing, and she discovered she could speak more freely. She even found the strength to prop herself up on the bed using her right arm as a lever.

"Do you know him?" asked Zed, his blue eyes sparkling. "He's brilliant – a genius!"

"I've met him."

"So, you know about his wonderful plan to change the world?"

"I'm aware of it."

"So, what is the best part of it, in your opinion? I'm interested. I'm sort of a student of him. A fan. More than a fan – I'm involved as well. Just like you." He gave a conspiratorial wink.

Rachel struggled to think. "Well, he's certainly organised."

"Samyaza, organised? I like it. What else?"

"Well, he wants to make changes – a lot of changes."

"Yes. Yes, he does. Anything else?"

Rachel stared around her, noticing that there were now a dozen small boys standing in a huddle near her bed. It threw her off her stride, and she fumbled for words.

Zed sighed. "It's okay. I was hoping to find out more from you. The thing is, he doesn't really let me know the details of his plan either. I'm not surprised you don't know anything worth knowing. It's okay. He is a genius, though, isn't he?"

"He's certainly ambitious," agreed Rachel. She plucked up the courage to add, "Listen, no more tea, okay? There's no need for that. I'll be good."

"Well, if Samyaza's interested in you, he must value you. And I don't want to get into his bad books."

Rachel nodded.

"Enough talking now. I must get back to my work. The clock is ticking, after all. I'm sure my boys will look after you."

Rachel looked across the line of small black eyes staring back through unreadable faces. There were around twenty boys now, which meant the room was almost full.

Zed towered above them, looking like an unkempt school teacher with a class full of ragged urchins. He pushed his way through the back row towards the bedroom door.

Leaving it ajar, he went through the front room, to the basement door, and down the dark stairs. The Malkin waited patiently for him with glassy eyes and a fixed expression. She was two fingers away from completion.

THE MAN HAD SAID NOT to trust the Rescuer, thought Rachel, so the Rescuer was real. But meanwhile, he had drugged her with poisoned tea and surrounded her with bubble-headed alien babies. He'd sent for Samyaza, his master, and gone to work on something in the basement that was so evil it made her feel ill.

There really was only one option. She had to get away.

Rachel pushed herself up and slowly swung her legs to the floor. The crowd of Spawners moved ever so slightly closer to her. Unlike conventional children, who make a lot of noise, move incessantly, and act unpredictably, this group had been silent and motionless until now. The ripple of movement gave her cause for concern. Although they shifted unhurriedly, like tall reeds blowing in a breeze, she was greatly outnumbered and didn't want to make any sudden movements.

"Easy now, boys," she whispered. Then, a brain wave hit her. "Hey, can I see that gift there?"

The boy in the front row, the original one, raised his hand, arm outstretched, pivoting at the shoulder. She glanced at the brutal carcass and forced herself to smile. It made her stomach churn, and she was relieved she couldn't smell the stench.

"Mm. Nice," she said. "You hang onto that one for now. I've seen that one already. Now, how about all of you guys go and get me some more gifts? Maybe you could get one each? I love presents. You in the front; why don't you show them the way? Show them where you found this guy? How about it?"

The weird boys bristled and turned their heads slightly towards their primary brother. A sea of eyes focused on one fixed point. Then, without a word, they filed out noiselessly.

As the last one left, Rachel got up and followed them out, several paces behind.

THEY HAD LEFT the front door open, and the cellar door was closed. They hadn't bothered Zed. As she passed the kitchen, Rachel thought about taking something sharp. However, escape was her number one goal, and she didn't want to get trapped back there, so she hurried on.

Outside the house, Rachel saw the boys scattered across the granite plain beneath the extravagant sky. They were hunting creatures at the edges of the plateau, where the ground gave way to spiky blue and grey undergrowth.

Stealthily, she crept in the opposite direction, away from the path she had taken earlier. Leaving the house behind her and veering to the right, she quickly skipped over the hard ground, relishing her newfound freedom.

Her senses were coming back, and she could now feel the rock beneath her feet and smell the mountain air. Like old friends, her taste, smell, and even an aching in her body came back to remind her she was alive, not dreaming.

The stone plateau had a boundary marked by a sharp ledge that dropped down a metre or so. It made the house look like it was sitting in the middle of a large flat dish. Rachel looked back to see whether the Olm family had noticed her absence. Some of them trudged back to the house while the others were still searching for their kills.

Suddenly, she was spotted. She spun around and leapt off the ledge in a single bound, landing in a patch of blue weeds. Without hesitation, she scrambled to her feet and bolted across the foreign terrain, heading into the unknown. Far behind her, Zed's voice echoed, "Maggie! Maggie McKenzie! You come back here now." Then she saw the children, moving like a rolling wave, breaking and surging towards her. They had switched from hunting strange creatures to hunting her.

So she fled through this unbelievable world, dodging over dark crevices and leaping across streams the colour of dead roses. The mountains encircled her as she descended the foothills. Bizarre, jagged rocks still hovered in the air, and something new appeared—clusters of stones floating, spinning, and sometimes vanishing like flames snuffed out by the wind.

She knew she was running farther and farther away from the doorway back to her home and that she might be forever lost on this massive nightmare planet. But the thought of staying in Zed's custody, surrounded by his spawners, was even worse. She tripped over a protruding root and fell flat on her face, gasping as the ground beneath her opened up to reveal a deep, narrow fissure, a crack in the rocks that seemed to fall away into endless darkness. Another one loomed ahead. She was quickly running out of solid ground, and at her back was a relentless pack of hunters closing in.

Tears welled up in Rachel's eyes.

As she pushed herself up to her knees and back to her feet, she saw the boys behind her, quickly gaining ground. She raced off again.

Rachel bounded over the gaps that opened up beneath her. Somehow, she found firm footing amongst the dry rock and the scrub. She was still descending the mountain foothills, which gave her a speed advantage. But this was also shared by the group behind, which bounced across the ground like a pack of lithe wolf cubs.

With dread, she noticed their numbers had swelled—what had started as thirty or forty Spawners had grown to nearly a hundred. They had fanned out, with those on the edges trying to outflank her. The tide of Spawners coming straight for her. She heard loose pebbles moving under a hundred pairs of feet.

Rachel started to sob as dark thoughts flooded her mind. The fear took hold. She felt certain that any minute, they would overtake her, pounce on her, and do something horrible to her, like eat her brains or spill her guts like that repulsive dead lizard. Panic hit her as she skidded to an abrupt halt. She couldn't go forward anymore. Rachel had come to the edge of a massive drop, a canyon that plunged into the heart of the ground where she now stood. A cold mountain wind whipped across her face, chilling her to the bone as she stared at the chasm.

With tears splashing on her clothes, Rachel desperately searched for a way down into the cavernous hole, but there were no walkways or footholds that would help her escape. She knew she would be captured again, drugged with that wretched tea, or worse, and forced to endure Samyaza once more. She didn't want them to hurt her. Now that her senses had come back, she knew that pain was her real enemy.

Overwhelmed, Rachel collapsed onto the rocky edge of the precipice and wrapped her arms around herself, hearing her pursuers approaching. As she rocked herself, she said quietly, into the thin air in front of her, "Rescuer, if you really are my rescuer, I need you right now."

CHAPTER 4

Zed stepped as close to the canyon edge as he dared. He had just watched the girl fall over the edge and tumble into the depths, dropping out of sight. He shook his head and grinned.

"Shame. Shame. Nice girl. Dead girl. Let's hope Samyaza's not too concerned, or I'll be a dead Zed, a big fat zero." He chuckled at his own joke as the wind ruffled his flyaway grey hair. Then, suddenly, his expression turned serious.

A sea of pale boys ebbed and flowed at his waist, noiselessly watching to see where Rachel had gone. They stared at each other from time to time in silent communication. Their heads bobbed up and down as they each took turns to peek over the edge.

A vast expanse opened up before them, with the edge of the opposite canyon wall in the distance. A verdant valley beyond it stretched to meet a series of caves and mountains. Beyond them was a desolate wasteland, a dry desert that stretched endlessly into the horizon.

"No, boys, she's gone. I know you wanted to play with her. If you like, we could go down the long way later and see if her body's still there. We could take the winding path through the valley. Maybe see if there's some hair or teeth we could salvage for our work? No, she's gone now. Nothing we can do. I have Samyaza on my mind. I need to get word to him not to hurry. In fact, he doesn't even need to come anymore. After all, I must finish my work, and I don't need him watching over my shoulder."

"Yes, of course, some of you can stay here and keep a-lookin'. But you know, the clocks a-tickin', and I have work to do."

With that, Zed turned and walked slowly back toward the house, across the long expanse of ground between the abyss and the black stone plateau. Soon, he was a tiny figure on a massive rocky plain with a house at one end and a sheer drop at the other, populated by a crowd of odd-looking children holding a silent vigil.

EDDIE SHOWERED AND SHAVED. He towelled off and pulled on some clothes. Then he chomped through a couple of slices of cold pizza from the fridge. It was barbecue chicken pizza with peppers and onions, even tastier than two days ago when it had been delivered hot.

He picked up his keys, wallet, and jacket, and before long, he was in his car, heading north to Lower Ledge Crossing. His instructions had been sparse but clear.

The roads were quiet, it being Sunday. According to his instructions, he found a place to park at Griffton Cliff, got out, and walked the rest of the way to the top. The Cliff was deserted, and a cool wind blew down from the overcast sky, whistling gently in his ears.

It was the first time he had seen the stone head in real life. It looked like something from a film set or Disney World. It sat upright, larger than a man, immovable and domineering. When the voice in his head commanded him to walk through it, he was sure he had lost his mind.

"That doesn't make any sense. What I do know is people get zapped if they try."

He shrugged. Maybe it would be the only way to bring this nightmare to an end.

What he didn't expect was for the structure to yield on impact.

Regardless, he ran at it with his big arms folded in front of him for protection, only willing to bruise his forearms. Eddie grunted as he collided with the stone head. A split second later, he was in the mezzanine world, gawping at a violet sky and a rolling, red-topped mountain range.

12345

RACHEL HELD her breath as she plummeted through the deep canyon. She passed broad strips of rock that flashed before her eyes in varying shades of brown and red. Long seconds passed before her body came to a sudden, jarring halt.

Some sort of safety net had checked her fall, though her body jerked horribly as it landed. It felt like a bed made of fist-sized rocks. They pressed into her spine, legs, and shoulders. The rocks disintegrated, and she fell once more. As her head dropped back, she saw the stones disperse above her as brown, grey, and red ribbons flashed in front of her eyes again. She was falling uncontrollably, gripped by a fear so intense it blanked her mind.

A second web stopped her descent once more. These stones felt smaller and had more give in them. Like a rag-doll thrown onto a mattress, she bounced, her arms and legs flailing wildly. This time, her body felt as though it had been pelted with hailstones. The rocky membrane gave way, and she dropped again, even further into the canyon. She could see the mouth of the canyon above her receding as she tumbled. There was no sign of her pursuers, and she assumed they had given her up for dead.

A third bed of rocks checked her fall. Then a fourth, then a fifth. After that, she lost count, bombarded by tiny stones, her body arrested again and again by the G-force and the harsh impact of the pebbles beneath her. She felt the pain of a thousand knobbly stones searing her skin.

Exhausted, she fell the rest of the way down the gully, crashing into the surface of a large body of water and slipping quickly into its embrace.

Her momentum pulled her down quickly into the depths. She felt the crushing pressure of the water on her whole body. It was shockingly cold.

As she sank, a voice echoed in her mind, "Come and find me. Now's the time. Come." They were the soothing and sonorous tones of a young man with a rich and humorous voice.

"How am I going to find you? I'm dead already," thought Rachel.

In seconds, she was deep underwater. She panicked, thrashing her limbs. It felt like the water was entering her mouth and lungs, filling her ears and flooding her brain. Everything went black.

EDDIE STUMBLED across the rocky terrain. He was in an open space, a valley with tall mountains in the distance.

The pinks and purples of this world amazed him as he recalled reading science fiction books in his youth about Mars exploration. Back then, before they'd even put a person on Mars, writers envisaged the shades of red that filled that alien world.

Several Mars explorers had sent back impressive pictures. Still, it wasn't until the first woman saw it with her own eyes a couple of years back that mankind felt they had really been there.

He felt just like that astronaut. Here he was, staggering beneath a swirling, veinous sky with a blood-red moon or sun, or perhaps it was Mars, looking large as life. Claret-red rocks and beetroot streams surrounded him as he snaked across the basin, leaping like a child.

He hoped he'd picked the right direction, having found the stone doorway close to him. It seemed the most logical choice, as the other direction opened into a barren rock desert without clear points of interest. No, he wouldn't last half an hour in that direction. He calculated this path had more hiding places in case a dinosaur came at him.

A lover of science fiction and an amateur writer of old, Eddie enjoyed the irony of the stone head, which gave passage to this world though seeming so solid and austere.

Since his arrival in this crazy place, he'd enjoyed all the unusual things that vied for his attention: bizarre and twisted trees and rocks that levitated above the ground, mammoth forests, and the sinewy magenta clouds that stretched across the sky. It was like nothing he could have envisioned or crafted in his wildest attempts at fiction.

Something was happening to Eddie Race. The experience was of a man waking up from his stupor. He already knew the reality of the other world, having encountered Samyaza on several occasions while seeking solace in the darkness, trying to contact his dead wife through mediums out of desperation and loneliness.

That was when the demon lord had taken hold of his life, insisting on being his 'forever friend.' Eddie knew Samyaza and his world on a purely visceral level but had never dreamt that such a world as this existed.

The voice in his head told him to keep going through the valley until he came to a house. But so far, there didn't seem to be any people, let alone a house. Nevertheless, he followed his orders and kept walking, enjoying the strange beauty of the landscape and relishing the exploration.

The ground could swallow Griffton up for all he cared, with all its problems and bad memories. What he needed was a fresh start. He could do with a house on a mountain beneath a purple sky.

In the far distance, he spied an angular construction amidst the rocks. It looked like a house. Eddie made a noise in his throat and pressed on.

Eventually, he reached it. The house was built on a plateau of black rock, which looked to Eddie like cooled lava or even solid obsidian.

"So, what do you want me to do, Samyaza?" he asked as he approached the building. The voice in his head fell silent.

Eddie braced himself and knocked at the front door, a weather-worn wooden construction with scuff marks at the base where it had been repeatedly kicked open.

The red-faced man who opened it was instantly apologetic, rubbing his dirty hands together and avoiding Eddie's gaze. It gave him the bravado to stand tall and face the stranger.

"Master, forgive me," the man said in a deep, throaty voice.

"What for?" Eddie asked, unsure.

"Ah, come in, do. I am just about to send off the Calloskira. The Malkin is almost complete, master. We're on track. Come in."

"Err," Eddie stammered, unsure of what he had just walked into.

"Zaelaza, you remember? They call me Zed."

Eddie followed Zed into the belly of his house, a monochrome affair in browns and greys. A small boy stood by the wall. On reflection, if it was a boy, it wasn't like any boy he'd ever seen. This one had a deathly pale face, bony limbs, and small, dark, beady eyes that reminded Eddie of a bird's.

"My son," said Zed in explanation. "Please, take a seat, master."

Eddie walked over and sat on an uncomfortable little sofa, his large body filling it completely. He shifted awkwardly, feeling out of place.

"Come in, Calloskira," Zed called, opening a door at the side of the room. A small, dark creature scuttled in. The creature was part spider-monkey and part bat. It had leathery black wings and displayed its fangs as it scurried along the floor.

"I'm sending the Calloskira to gather the final pieces now that we have located their owners. There is one in Poland, a boy, and one in China, a girl, as you know."

Eddie had no clue what he was talking about.

"I want you to know, master, that we are still very much on schedule. The Malkin will be finished, and she will be triumphant. You can be sure of that. I am grateful for my part in it all, of course, and I have you to thank for choosing me. If there is anything else you need me to do, just let me know—especially when you come into your kingdom. Know that I am your humble servant always."

Zed walked over to the door and opened it for the bat-like creature. With a screech and a flutter of reptilian wings, the Calloskira launched powerfully into the skies and soared into the clouds. Eddie got up from his chair to watch it from the doorway, raising his eyebrows.

"He knows the way out," Zed said reassuringly.

"Out?" said Eddie.

"Yes. Into the world."

After that, Eddie stayed quiet for a while, trying to bend his mind around the strange things he was hearing and seeing.

"Tea?" asked Zed. Eddie shook his head.

"I know what you're going to ask me, master. The girl, yes? The one I sent word to you about?"

"Girl?" Eddie asked, confused.

"Please don't harm me. I did my best, master. The girl ran. She fell. There was nothing we could do. Please. I'm just a humble craftsman. Your servant."

"Hold on. What girl?"

"Her name's Maggie. Maggie McKenzie. She's a teenager, I suppose you'd call her. Small with black hair. Oh, and one finger missing. Not my doing, though. She was like that when she arrived."

Eddie froze. "Come again?"

"The finger, like the Malkin. Only, the Malkin's missing two fingers, but she's nearly complete. Just trust me to finish the job."

"Which hand?" Eddie cut in.

"The girl? Her left one."

"Which way did she go?"

"I'm so sorry. It's no use. She's dead."

"Which way did she go? Show me."

"I'll take you there. But first, wouldn't you like to see the Malkin? She's my best work, the best I've ever done in all my days. A masterpiece. A beauty." Zed waved his arms dramatically and smiled a proud smile.

It suddenly hit Eddie like a freight train. *Maggie McKenzie.* That name was familiar. It was the name of a distant cousin on his mother's side. Margaret McKenzie, or Aunt Margaret, is what he and Rachel used to call her. She was an older woman with yellow teeth who enjoyed chewing Garibaldi biscuits and laughed like a horse.

"Take me to the girl," Eddie demanded, his voice hardening.

CHAPTER 5

Rachel came to her senses at the side of a large lake. Groggy and wet, she thought at first that she was back in Griffton, by the sea. But then she realised the water wasn't moving in the same way. The tide at Griffton Beach hissed and snaked along the sand. This one just sort of sat there and made tiny lapping sounds. It was far more tranquil here. For starters, there were no seagulls squawking.

Then she saw the brown canyon walls in the distance and, high above her head, the swirling sky the colour of violets and amethysts. Between her and the purple canopy, individual rocks and whole groups of stones hung in midair, fading in and out. Incredibly, they had broken her fall and kept her from dying. It had been no less than miraculous.

"Thank you, rocks," she said. They winked in and out of existence as though in acknowledgement.

Oddly, she felt at peace. She wasn't being attacked, and she was alive.

She lay on a soft, dry mud bank that sloped down to the water's edge. It really was a beautiful lake, crystal-clear at its closest point and dark blue out towards the depths. In places, the water took on the brown and grey hues of the canyon's rock walls. Towards the edges, she could see the reflection of the trees that dotted the banks. There was also some low-lying vegetation around the lake, plants with blue and green wispy fronds or elongated leaves that drooped over the water.

Somewhere behind her, she could hear the faint sound of a waterfall hissing ceaselessly. Apart from that, all was quiet.

After a while, she got up, checked that she was in one piece, and set off to investigate. She was soaking wet, but it didn't feel like a problem. After all, she was alive, and those horrid nightmare creatures were far behind. The red sun above sent down warm rays, and her skin absorbed these happily.

"Come and find me," the voice had said.

The bank sloped up towards a trail leading to a distant part of the canyon. She couldn't see far beyond the shrubs and trees close at hand but soon found herself weaving through the maze of blue branches and tendrils.

An inexpressible joy filled her heart, and she laughed at her most recent adventure at Zed's house.

Sure, he had drugged her, but it was only to keep her put. She even found the little boy and his brothers amusing. They liked her, so they brought her dead things. Cats do it all the time.

Then she thought about Lake Emerson. Of course, he messed up frequently, but he made her laugh. Real life was serious, but somehow, he always saw the funny side and knew how to turn a frown into a smile. Whether it was sticking something ridiculous up his nose—a chip or a marshmallow—or pulling a goofy face, or cracking one of his terrible jokes. But it always did the trick, and that's what she needed. If he had decided to take off with Kumiko, the Hello Kitty princess, then Rachel had to admit she was partly to blame for pushing him away.

Then there was Iona. She was drawn to her because, like Lake, Iona took life lightly and knew how to transform an ordinary evening into a special occasion with candles, music, intrigue, and fun. Unlike her, both Iona and Lake knew how to skate over the surface of this dark world. She was always so serious! She burst out laughing, unable to keep her elation from manifesting itself. She wondered what was wrong with her. Was she going crazy?

Rachel forced herself to be serious and grew solemn again. The world was changing, she reflected. Back in Griffton, the medieval warrior men had taken over Daniel's house, and the strange stone head had landed. Things were definitely changing at home. Her father had gone from being a happy family man to a monster who was no fun to be with. He was a grumpy, non-communicative, angry brute. Everything was going wrong, falling apart and falling away. There was no hope left in Griffton.

But still, she felt this inexplicable joy, a lightness in the depths of her very self, north of her stomach and south of her neck, somewhere near her heart.

The sound of the waterfall had grown louder, and she skipped over a stream that was growing in size and volume as she walked. She wondered if it fed an underground tributary that joined the lake. She had learned about that in geography.

Glassy rivulets sparkled beside her. Lost in thought, Rachel scrambled over loose stones and leapt from rock to rock. It was warmer now, and she was enjoying her explorations.

Suddenly, she came upon it.

The magnificent waterfall roared in front of her, its relentless streams of water cascading down the rocks and filling a deep, clear pool. The torrent fell into a colossal, circular stone basin that looked as if it had been hand-carved for the purpose.

Rachel climbed closer to the rocky bowl and raised her eyes to follow the waterfall skywards. It fell from such a height that the top was lost from view. The noise of rushing water filled her head as she watched it foam and froth at the bottom, feeling cool droplets of water tickling her face.

Unable to contain herself, she kicked off her damp trainers, ripped off her socks and jeans, and hauled herself up to the lip of the round basin. It was probably reckless, but she felt safe, drawn by an irresistible urge to splash about in the water. Being a Griffton girl, she was used to jumping into the sea at the drop of a hat, no matter how cold it was.

Seconds later, she was kicking her legs and waving her arms under the curtain of water that fell from above. To her surprise, it was much warmer than she expected, as though it had been heated by hot springs. She had heard about places with naturally hot water, like the famous springs in Banff, Canada, that people travelled miles to experience.

The joy in her heart welled up, almost to bursting point. The more she dove under the surface and floated in the deep, cavernous stone basin, the more refreshed she felt. She declared to herself that this was her place, her sanctuary, and she had discovered it all on her own.

"I name you Rachel's Pool," she said, giggling and floating on her back. She cast her gaze up at the warm red sun. The sky had a violet hue, tinted in places with magenta swirls. It was reminiscent of raspberry ripple ice cream.

Rachel hummed a tune and then sang a light and carefree— a made-up melody that bubbled from her like a child's. She giggled again. It felt like the time she had encountered the Dunamis in the house up at Griffton Cliff with Lake and Caleb Noble, the adventurer. Her body had buzzed with electricity, and her heart had swelled like a foaming wave. It was so pleasurable to experience it again; she thought she never would, that it had been a creation of her mind and emotions: a function of being rescued from that dank prison cell.

"This place isn't bad at all," she murmured.

A voice replied, rising above the constant roar of the waterfall. "Do you like it? It's one of my favourites."

Startled, Rachel saw a young man sitting on the rocks nearby. He was muscular, with long white hair and a handsome face. A simple platinum crown rested on his head, and he wore light armour over a long white tunic. When he looked at her, his eyes shone like the sun. Rachel grabbed the stone ledge and tried to hide her body completely behind it. Her heart was beating so fast she thought she might pass out. But she finally took a deep breath, steadying herself, and gathered the courage to look at the man again. He was waiting patiently, not staring, but obviously keen to talk.

"I have brought you a fresh towel and a change of clothes. And then I have some food for you just over there," he said, gesturing to a spot nearby.

"For me?" she asked, still gawking, her legs treading water.

"Yes, Rachel. I'd like to spend time with you."

Her mind spun as she clung to the ledge. "With me? You want to spend time with me?"

"I'll go and check on my horse while you get ready," he added calmly. "Come and find me when you're ready."

And with that, he stood up and walked away, leaving Rachel floating in the pool, completely bewildered.

RACHEL FIDGETED and looked down at her lap. She really liked the simple pale green dress she was wearing, and it fit perfectly. It had a thin golden hem, beautifully embroidered. While they felt comfortable against her skin, she didn't feel comfortable at all. She was invited to sit and sample whatever she fancied from a broad, natural stone table. After piling her earthenware plate with colourful salad, vegetables, cheeses, and slices of interesting bread, she sat on a mossy stone seat and felt miserably inadequate. He was so powerful and different from her. He seemed pure, like the water in the stone bowl. Confidence, gentleness, and grace marked his movements.

The man's long sword rested against his muscular leg, sheathed in a dark scabbard. She tried not to stare at his thigh tattoo as his tunic swished. He helped himself to some food, possibly just to keep her company. Confident and majestic, his very presence made her feel wretched inside. Then he turned to smile at her, and her heart soared. Everything was okay, and she was safe. The memory resurfaced—last week's dream in her hospital bed, where she had sat with the Rescuer King and his warriors, listening to his tales under a purple sky.

"Relax. Eat," he said.

They ate in silence, listening to the sound of the waterfall. Rachel had a metal goblet filled with sweet-tasting iced water. The canyon's high walls hung over them, with brown and grey layers rising into the sky.

They were in a raised, clear area close to the wall. The sun warmed them as they sat at their stone table, which gave a view over the rocky path accompanying the stream back through the trees.

Rachel was awash with questions but could not ask, bound by fear or shame. She frowned a little, concentrating on her mouthful.

He waited for her to finish eating and said, "So, say you got to meet your maker face to face. What would you ask him?"

Rachel laughed from her throat and looked to one side of the Rescuer's face. Streams of water cascaded down the rocks and into the pool below, their gentle rhythm filling the air.

"Aha. There is no maker. Everyone knows that."

"I see." He smiled, taking a bite from a large ripe plum.

Rachel continued, "Well, that was what I was always taught at school anyway. Religion is a disease, a thing of the past. It causes too many wars and stuff. So, they, like, destroyed all the holy books and locked up all those mad people to protect us. Or maybe they killed them, I forget which. It all happened a few years before I was born, to be honest, so I don't really think about it. But I do know that faith is dangerous and deludes people," declared Rachel. "That's what they told us anyway."

"You don't really believe that, do you? After what you've seen?" There was a pause, and then Rachel blurted out, "Rescuer, what's my purpose? What's my life for?"

The Rescuer smiled gently. "Your purpose is to love me and

live with me in your life: your rescuer, your creator, the lover of your soul."

"But I don't even know you."

"Well, now you do. Here I am, pleased to meet you!" He held out a hand, his eyes warm and inviting. Rachel stared at it as though he were offering her a loaded gun. After a hesitant moment, she placed her small hand in his and felt the warmth of his skin. A surge of electric currents coursed through her.

In explanation, the Rescuer said, "I stand in the gap, holding the hand of man, holding the hand of the Creator who dwells in unapproachable light." He let go of Rachel's hand, leaving her reeling and awestruck. Her palm buzzed with static.

He leant back and laughed, but not unkindly, then lifted his metal goblet and drank deeply. "Why don't you sit back and allow me to tell you a story or two?"

"Okay. I'd like that." Rachel wriggled and got herself comfortable in her moss-covered chair.

"There was an artist who painted many great works of art, masterpieces in many people's estimation. One was of a beautiful waterfall with a glittering torrent that splashed on the rocks and filled a pool to overflowing. Rachel's Pool, they called it."

Rachel smiled.

"Another painting was of a fiery-red desert sunset that touched the tips of the dunes with rosy flames. The paint he applied so thickly with his palette knife that it looked like buttery ice cream you could eat with a spoon. His colours were vibrant and textured, wild and alive.

"But one day, he realised one of his masterpieces was missing from his house. It had a place in his favourite room where he relaxed and passed the time. He searched everywhere for it, lifting canvasses and looking through all of his possessions but in vain, for he soon learnt that it was hanging on the wall in the house of a thief.

"Marching over to the house of that villain, he forced open the door and searched the house until he found his masterpiece

– his creation. The painting was of a stunning young girl with gorgeous light brown skin, black hair, and huge brown eyes." The Rescuer looked Rachel in the face. She held his gaze for a moment, then looked away.

"Although he loved all of his masterpieces without a doubt, this was one of his prized possessions, and he just could not live without it in his life. That very day, he fetched back that beautiful picture and returned it to his house, where it belonged."

He paused and took a sip of his water. Rachel inhaled and sat silently. "Would you like another story?"

Rachel nodded thoughtfully. She was enjoying the rhythm of the voice of the King and his deep tones.

"There was a small girl who wandered far away from her father's house when she was just a child. It was an accident and not really her fault, as she followed a purple butterfly across the hills. But it led her far away, into the sunset and into the night, and the butterfly was lost to her.

"Realising she was alone now and unable to find her father's house again, she lay down in a warm ditch and settled into the leaves. They provided a soft bed and some respite from the unfamiliar world she had found herself in. Cradled there, she fell asleep. She grew older and never gave up searching for home. She learned to sleep in the leaves or dirt by the side of the road and eventually found another father.

"The problem was that he was a tyrant who either beat or ignored her, and every night she cried herself to sleep. After a very long while, she came to believe that this was what a real father was like, and she forgot about her father, who loved her.

"Meanwhile, her real father was looking for her daily, searching the roads and every house; her father who loved her and would die for her. One day, he found her hanging washing in the garden of a stranger. When he saw her, he threw his arms around her and wept on her shoulder, together at last.

"When the stranger showed his face, her father overpowered him and led her home without delay. You see, every moment is precious between a loving father and his daughter who loves him. She returned home, safe at last."

Rachel felt the soft tears trickling down her cheeks, but she continued to listen. His soothing words were a balm to her ears and her weary spirit, calming the storm inside her.

"Would you like one last story?" said the Rescuer. Rachel nodded.

"This story is about a girl who enjoyed playing on the beach with her bucket and spade. She played until the sun went down, building great castles made of wet sand. She played until the tide drew back, making the beach a broad expanse.

"At the end of the day, all the families were packing their belongings and putting away their own chairs and buckets and spades. One by one, they left the beach for the warmth of their homes: mothers, fathers, children, and grandparents.

"Only, the little girl was nowhere to be found, and her father was growing anxious as he cast his eyes along the beach and over the waves. Ceaselessly, he searched for her. He never stopped looking. Near the cars, then out to sea, where the shore had grown to reveal a desert of sand. But she was nowhere to be found.

"He drove his car along the beach, end to end, then up and down, calling out for her all the while, crying out and hunting for his little girl. He waded far into the depths, crying out for her, but heard nothing in return.

"He went looking for her for what was left of that long day and well into the night. The moon came out to keep him company as he made the lonely, desperate search over and over again, but she was lost to him.

"And then he saw her, his darling girl, lying under an abandoned deckchair, fast asleep. The roar of release and delight that came from his throat was like the thundering of a waterfall. He'd found his child, his beloved one, the apple of his eye."

Rachel wept quietly.

"And so, Rachel, have I found you."

CHAPTER 6

"Who are you really?" asked Rachel. "I feel in my heart that you are good, and I can see that you're really here with me, if I really am here, that is. But I sense you're very different from me or anyone or anything I've ever known. Perfect, in fact. So, who are you?" She knew she was babbling.

"I have many names."

As he spoke, his eyes flamed like fire, and his voice resonated with the sound of many rushing streams. His countenance began to glow brighter and brighter.

"I am the Rescuer, the Living One, the Bright Morning Star. I am the First and the Last, the Beginning and the End, a ransom for many. I make all things new, and that includes you, Rachel."

She listened and then hung her head. "That's what I want. I want to be new again. I want it more than anything. But how can that possibly happen? You don't know my life. You don't know who I am and what I've done." She looked up at him and added, "Or do you?"

His face started to shine like the sun, and Rachel gasped and fell to her knees.

"I know you intimately, Rachel Isabelle Race. I knew you before you were born. I know things about you, but no one knows. I know how much it hurt when your mother died and how you used to cut yourself to let the pain out. I know these things, Rachel, and I care about you deeply and completely."

Rachel collapsed onto her hands, sobbing uncontrollably. The weight of everything crashed down on her as her tears fell freely onto the ground. She cried out, "Why did you let her die, Rescuer? Why did she have to die? Why couldn't you save her?"

The sound of the waterfall thundered in her ears.

"I loved your mother very much, Rachel, but I also needed her. In her life, she knew me, and I knew her, and we were close. But it was time to call her home. She may be dead in your world, but in mine, she's alive. I'm not asking you to understand; I know how hard it was. How hard it still is: I understand. But she's with me now, in a place where there is life."

Rachel wailed. The sound of her cries filled the canyon.

"I can help you heal, Rachel. Walk with me, and I will walk with you from now on if you want me to. Are you ready? Will you trust me? Will you be friends with me?"

"How can I be friends with a King? You don't know what I've done. You don't know about my life. There's nothing good about me," wailed Rachel.

"Don't be afraid. I know all things, and I have the power to forgive. It's time for a fresh start, dear one. Trust me. Follow me," said the sound of rushing water.

Rachel started to feel warmth in her heart. It felt as though there was a small flame flickering. A wriggly worm of fire tickled her insides.

"What's happening to me, Rescuer?" Rachel had panic in her voice. With fear and awe, she stared up at the blazing figure in front of her, who was emitting the light of the sun. A furnace kicked into life, heating her from the inside.

"Relax and allow the Dunamis to do his work," said the Rescuer.

Simultaneously, the Dunamis said, "Relax, Rachel Race, and trust me."

Slowly, memories started to come to her mind, highlighting her fears and anxieties, her secret shame and hidden desires. They came unrushed, to begin with, but soon gathered pace.

Soon, the memories were like a mountain wind blasting her body. The blazing fire in her heart revealed the angry core that tore at her soul, wrapped in a shell of selfishness and pride. Her independent soul danced and scowled, lit up by the fire inside. It glowered at the Rescuer, burning under the relentless fire of the Dunamis. Drenched with hatred towards her maker, Rachel's soul bristled.

"For us to be close, all of this must be dealt with," said the Rescuer, his voice coming from far away. "Let me exchange your poison for my purity?"

Rachel assented. Suddenly, the fire in her heart spread across her body, and she felt her veins and bones turn to liquid fire. Lying on the ground now, she screeched, a long and hollow sound that spoke of desperation and pain. It seared her frame, burning her from the inside. Excruciating pain, raw, naked pain, pulsed through her body, sending her rolling, shrieking, and howling across the ground.

She had no words for this experience but felt like she was an onion being peeled layer by layer, right down to its core. No stone was left unturned as the fire revealed her rage, shame, blame, manipulation, and resentment; she had no idea it was all in there—a noxious cocktail of poison.

"I'm sorry! Forgive me, Rescuer? I'm sorry," she sobbed. "Take it away! Take it all away."

The heat touched them all in turn, bringing them back into line, under submission, incinerating the chaff.

Like gold being refined, she felt her impurities burning off, devoured, and consumed by the liquid fire within. The operation lasted a few seconds, though it felt like an eternity.

Just as suddenly as it had come upon her, the mighty flame

died down, leaving a warm glow in her heart. She rested there in a daze. She felt recalibrated, purified, and forgiven. She lay still on the ground, face up, arms limp by her sides.

There had been a monumental shift in the universe. Nothing would be the same again. She was clean, pure, and blameless before her Rescuer, fit to be friends with the King of all things. Unfamiliar emotions flowed through her: relief, peace, freedom.

She wept for losing her mother but with pure tears, devoid of bitterness or desperation or rage, for the first time in her life.

She no longer cried with sadness but with a fond love and an acceptance that was entirely new to her. She felt as though the fire had healed her heart.

Rachel found herself laughing, her body shaking, and a fresh wave of tears emerged. Her heart reflected the afterglow of the fire and remained warm. Her limbs buzzed with electricity.

After a long time, she stood to her feet, feeling a new sense of peace in her body.

"Rescuer?" she called out. She turned around, feeling energised. Her limbs were strong and vibrant. She saw the waterfall, the pool, and the path down to the forest. The canyon walls towered above, and solitary trees edged the stone basin.

The King was nowhere to be seen, but as she stood, feet apart, back straight, she felt the power of the Rescuer's Dunamis living inside her.

There was a new feeling in her heart, a passionate love that burned with a mighty flame. She felt she was loved with a jealous love, the love of the Creator for his creature.

He had chosen her and loved her, his daughter, fiercely. And so, she felt love for the one who had rescued her, her creator, the lover of her soul.

"THIS IS WHERE SHE FELL," said Zed.

Eddie squinted and peered over the edge of the canyon.

There was a sheer drop that plunged straight down, ending with a broad lake at the bottom. It made his stomach lurch.

"She fell down there?"

"That's right." Zed grinned. However, the expression on his albino son's face didn't change. He just stared with hard, black eyes like lumps of coal.

"What are you grinning about?" Eddie snapped.

"Oh, you know, just the comedy of life and the tragedy of life. Easy come, easy go, here today, gone tomorrow. You always say, Master Samyaza, that humans are so weak."

Eddie stared out across the gap, wheezing. "What did you just call me?"

"Master?" Zed asked in a confused tone. "You are my master, aren't you? In this big man's body?"

Eddie took a deep breath, turned to the man, and spat, "Samyaza is a lying, manipulative, evil, scheming…"

"Oh, so you're not my master," Zed snarled.

"I most certainly am not. My name is Eddie Race, and that young girl, Maggie, is my daughter, Rachel."

"Oh, I see. My mistake. So, my Malkin and my Calloskira are both unknown to you? Okay. I see."

He turned to the young boy. "Sweet Olm. He's all yours." With that, Zed walked away.

Eddie had a split second to realise that the albino boy had rushed headlong into his stomach, pushing him, with all his might, over the edge of the canyon.

THE LAKE SPARKLED, the distant waterfall whispered, and Rachel Race felt alive, bulletproof, in fact. She was back at the water's edge, dressed in her own clothes again, sitting on the bank and gazing across the lake's smooth surface. It was so calm here. Peace seemed to radiate through the air like a wide, invisible wave that bathed her with tranquillity.

She was getting used to the feeling of having the Dunamis with her. This powerful presence accompanied and protected her. She had been cut from fire, carved from the flames, and her reward was this peace far beyond her understanding.

The breeze blew the leaves of an elegant plant that dangled over the surface of the water.

Suddenly, there was a great splash at the centre of the lake, sending angry ripples toward the edges. Startled, Rachel stared at the point of entry. Something, or someone, had nosedived into the water. Could it have been Zed or one of his alien boys?

She stood up, her mind made up in an instant, and leapt into the lake, fully clothed. Whoever had fallen in—whether it was Zed or another inhabitant of this strange land—didn't deserve to die for nothing. If it was someone else, perhaps they could help her escape. But first, she had to rescue them.

Invigorated by the cold water, she swam toward where she thought the person had fallen. She searched for signs of life. Her heart raced as she spotted thrashing arms, movements slowing in the thick water. She dove beneath the surface, searching until her eyes caught sight of a man sinking slowly. It was her father.

Being a strong swimmer and trained in lifesaving, both at the pool and in the sea, Rachel shifted into automatic and grabbed his body. Kicking hard, she dragged him up to the surface. With more powerful moves, she brought him to the bank. She spent the last of her energy hauling his large body onto the muddy shore, her eyes intense and her mouth a long, determined line.

She had acted just in time. Eddie lay, spluttering and cough-ing, facedown at the edge of the lake. As he came to himself, he took one look at her and began to sob. His words were a jumbled mess, and Rachel let him ramble, cradling his head in her lap.

"Rachel! My girl! Did he hurt ya? I didn't mean for things to…" he said.

"Daddy! My daddy," Rachel cried. She saw him for the first

time as a wounded soul: a hurting man carrying the weight of the world on his shoulders. It wasn't his fault he didn't know how to talk to her about his feelings. It was just hard for him. Until now, that was.

Weeping like a baby, he started to pour out his heart. "My baby. You're alive! I'm so sorry. I was never there for you. I was so worried you were gone forever. I couldn't live without you. I'm sorry I broke your presents that Christmas."

As his disorderly thoughts tumbled out in non-sequiturs and staccato phrases, Rachel learned how terrified he had been of losing her, how he had been led into this underworld by Samyaza, and how much regret and fear he carried with him.

Rachel listened patiently to everything he needed to say. All the while, she cradled him in her arms, rocking and cuddling him, saying she forgave him and understood.

While they communed, the Dunamis embraced them like a force field, uniting them and covering them with a blanket of peace.

They spent a long time in silence, just holding each other, a loving father and his daughter, making up for the years. Neither wanted to break away, and Eddie felt himself drifting into a peaceful slumber. Just as he began to doze, he gazed at Rachel and croaked, "Your hair. It's all white."

"Yeah, my hair's fine, Dad."

"No, not all right—I'm saying it's all white, like snow."

Rachel carefully laid his head on the ground and walked over to the water's edge. She gasped at her reflection. Her once dark hair was now silvery white, stark against her light brown skin and dark eyes.

She turned back to Eddie, but he was asleep. Standing beside him was the tall figure of the Rescuer, his face no longer glowing but rugged and handsome, as she remembered. He held a long rope, at the end of which was his chunky white steed, the one from Rachel's dream. She could hear the horse's breathing as it waited, gently tossing its head.

"My dear Edward."

"You know him?"

The Rescuer smiled. "I know him. I brought him here to complete your healing, Rachel. But I have chosen him too. It's his turn to be renewed, which is his heart's desire. But as you know, that is best done without an audience."

"Oh, okay. So, what about me?"

The Rescuer hauled Eddie up easily and carried him over to his horse, carefully placing his limp body over the saddle. Rachel marveled at his strength, though she had come to expect the extraordinary from him.

"You are ready now. Go. Your friends are past the waterfall and out through the valley. Follow the Dunamis and have faith in him. He will lead and protect you. In due course, you must face the Malkin, but all in good time."

With that, the Rescuer turned and began to walk away, leading Eddie and the stallion toward another part of the canyon.

"Can't I come with you?" she called out feebly, but the Rescuer kept walking, leading his grand stallion along the water's edge, carrying her father to who knows what kind of fire trial.

"Rachel, I'm with you now. I'll never leave you," she heard him say.

She smiled. Then she grinned, and soon, she was laughing and shaking her head. She took one last look at the muddy bank on which she had embraced her father, something she never dreamt she could do but had secretly longed for. With a lightness in her heart, she slowly made her way up the stream-covered path, heading toward the waterfall and beyond.

CHAPTER 7

"You know what, Lake? For someone who is no longer going out with Rachel Race, you certainly talk a lot about Rachel Race."

"Shut up, Harvey."

Harvey was another reporter at the Griffton News. He was tall and smug and had an annoying habit of stating the obvious and delivering it in an ironic tone. The paper liked him because he could do this in his written copy and in conversation.

"Which would, in fact, suggest that, despite the fact that this other girl, Kumiko, right? Despite the fact that this other girl is great looking and fun to be with, for some unknown reason, you would rather be with the aforementioned Rachel Race."

"Drop dead, Harvey."

"I just want you to be honest with yourself. Anyway, how long has it been since you and Rachel broke up?"

"Friday was the last time I saw her. Friday last week. We had a row. I left her somewhere in danger, I thought. She was being a lunatic, as usual. She wouldn't listen to reason."

Lake stared across the room as the conversation at the gates of Lytescote Manor filled his head. He could see himself standing just outside the gates and arguing with Rachel, who was adamant that she would be fine without him. However, Lake feared that Daniel Harcourt was a maniac who would do her harm. Oh well, it was her funeral. He expected them to find her in a shallow grave.

"You know what, Lake? If I really were your friend, I would walk you slowly out to the back of the building, load a gun, and do the decent thing: put you down like the sick horse you are."

"Ah, you're just – jealous."

"Of your life? You have got to be kidding me. To be honest with you, I've got trouble of my own. Spike Rewrite has got me following dead-end leads the whole day long."

"He used to do that to me, too, when I was new. Here's what I think he does. I think he dives down to the bottom of the slush pile, grabs a handful of last year's leads, and picks someone's desk at random. It just happened to be you. If you want my advice, Harvey, follow one of your own leads and do your own story. He won't know or care as long as you come up with the goods by press time."

"Thanks, *hombre*. And if you want my advice on the girl situation, trust me—I know girls—have some fun and forget about Rachel Race. Life's too short."

A heavy presence appeared at the door of the coffee room. It was Mike Wright, weighed down by the responsibility of monitoring a dozen wayward writers and editors, plus a muttering bank of production staff.

On top of this, he faced an increasingly irrational executive team intent on curbing his freedom to cover stories just in case they upset the shareholders or corporate sponsors. It was ridiculous; the country was meant to have a free press, for goodness' sake.

Mike said in a gruff voice, "Break's over, lads. Time and tide wait for no one, and neither do newspaper deadlines; more's the pity. How are those stories going?" It was more of a command than a question.

Harvey mumbled something and slunk back to his desk. Lake relaxed into his chair, letting his spine melt into the backrest. He slowly finished his coffee, placed the mug deliberately on the table, and then turned towards the door. His eyes were wet with tears. Rachel would be just fine without him, he thought. But would he be fine without Rachel?

There was no one at the door. Mike had left several minutes earlier to battle the firestorm of phone calls and the undying beast in his email inbox. Time and tide wait for no one, and an ocean of ink was poised to wash over the shores of next week's newspaper, ready to bring the stories to life.

Kumiko kicked back on the rollers of Daniel Harcourt's study chair, alone at last. Griffton's movers and shakers had all left the house, but it was still full of 'Sapana' Dream Warriors who used it as their home base. They had taken over almost every space in the house, apart from this one, sleeping many to a room and pillaging the store cupboards in the basement. She was happy to leave them to their own devices, gambling, cursing, and drilling each other in combat training to pass the time.

She kicked up her right leg and landed it on the desk. She was wearing a little black dress made of lace, with three-quarter-length sleeves and a pair of leopard print stilettos. Her heel landed next to an ornate Oriental pen holder.

She liked the quaint study but in the way that a child is curious about their great-grandfather's office, with its leather and wood and old-world smells. There is something delicious about finding a room in an unfamiliar house that's jam-packed with curiosities and oddities.

Her fingers tickled the desk and discovered a hidden drawer underneath, holding a fountain pen, a stick of red sealing wax, and a handful of foreign coins. She opened her mouth with delight.

Big old tomes lined the shelves in the study, rising on either side of a broad chimney breast, beneath which was the deep open fireplace. The fireplace was also a secret exit from the house that led down into the ground and through the woods.

That was how Daniel and his family had escaped, but it didn't really matter in the grand scheme of things because Samyaza had all his bases covered. Nothing would thwart his plans now: his strategy had the momentum of a swinging axe blade.

He spoke. "Kumiko. It's me."

"Samyaza," she whispered seductively. "Hey, I like this house. A girl could get used to this kind of living."

"Think of it as a present, an early reward for what we are about to achieve together over the next few days and weeks."

"Tell me more."

"All in good time, my dearest. What I can tell you is that later today, you will send out the teams of Sapanas and initiate the next phase. We have people in position, so once things move to the next level, the rest should fall into place easily."

"That sounds like fun. I don't need to know the details. I like surprises."

"That's my girl."

She gazed at her handsome young friend, who flirted with her in her mind's eye. He was a brown-skinned surfer with wavy black hair that fell to his shoulders and dark eyebrows that framed his attentive eyes.

"You know, Kumi, I've liked you as long as I've known you, and I watched you for quite a while before we met."

"Okay, that doesn't freak me out."

"I know it doesn't. I saw you when your parents moved you from school to school across the Pacific Rim as they swapped one military post for another. You went to two dozen schools in a dozen years, with jets overhead and jeeps on the ground."

"Yup, that's me, the army brat."

"I saw you making new friends at each place, spinning tales

about the past, confident that people only know what you tell them, and knowing they believed it all. You told some wonderful lies and broke many hearts."

Kumi smirked.

"But you liked your own company and kept them at a distance, didn't you? I noticed when your father died in combat and then your mother, the only family you had. I saw you unravelling, travelling, living off your wits and the naivety of strangers, people you secretly despised because they had something you didn't have: family."

Kumi's expression grew hard.

"Don't worry. It's not a crime to be angry about your life or bitter about it all. It's okay to be deathly unhappy deep down. Sometimes you hit the bottom, didn't you? But you always came back fighting. Kicking and punching. That's what I love about you, Kumiko."

Kumiko was quiet for a while, staring at the spines of the ancient books on the shelves. "But Samyaza, we've only really known each other for a few weeks, not even a month. Why all this talk about love?"

"Because I want to have adventures with you and rule the world with you. Because I love you, and you love me."

"I see."

"Tell me you love me. Tell me you adore me." The surfer boy looked Kumi square in the face, standing at the centre of her spirit and winking at her. His eyes were smouldering embers, his voice like nectar dripping from rose petals.

"I do," she said and folded her arms. "Just as I thought."

They both laughed.

After a pause, Samyaza said, "But you want someone with a physical body, don't you? I will be with you in due course, in body, and in spirit, you know that? But I understand. I could send you a helper in the interim. Someone you could work with."

"Oh, yes, that would be nice."

"Do you have any suggestions?"

"How about Lake?"

"Not him, surely? Don't you want someone better? Why don't you give me a better suggestion?"

"Oh, I don't know. Surely Lake will do?"

"All right, so be it. If that's what you want. So, my beautiful Kumi, we're on track. We stand on the brink of a battle, a historic war that will liberate the earth and alter it forever. It's time for them to experience me. We will be triumphant, you and I, ruling and reigning with the world beneath our feet."

"Why me?" asked Kumi.

"I thought I made that clear, or do you just want to hear it again?"

"I want to hear it again."

"All right then. You, my dear, are special. You are one in seven billion. You are my queen, and I am your king."

LAKE WORKED at a bank of desks occupied by other news reporters, feature writers, and a few of the section heads. The more important editors had their own desks on the far side of the wide room. The subeditors and art and design crew sat on the opposite side, near the kitchen. Lake was sitting at his computer. He looked around and tried to focus again. As usual, phones rang, people chatted, printers whirred, and papers rustled.

He tried calling Kumi and even fired off a couple of heavy-hearted texts, but she wasn't answering. It was late afternoon, and she still hadn't swung by as promised. It left him frustrated and alone, though his thoughts quickly went to Rachel. The phones had died down for the afternoon as commuters hit the road and the day's news stories caught their breath. The stories for the day had been set, and copy was almost ready to go.

Then it happened.

First, Mike's phone rang. The conversation seemed intense, Lake noted, as Mike's face turned grim and his eyes took on a glassy, distant look. Then, Lake's phone buzzed.

It was a contact near the army barracks on the outskirts of Griffton, near Polcombe. There had been some sort of explosion on the west side of town.

Mike and Lake quickly caught up with each other. "What do you know, Lake?"

"Not much. A huge bang and lots of smoke."

"Me too."

"Do you think it's an ammo dump? Any other explosions?" asked Mike.

"My contact doesn't know. What do you reckon? Sabotage or a terrorist attack?"

"Whatever it is, it's the top story now."

Mike turned around and addressed the room.

"Explosion at the military facility on the west side in the last five or ten minutes," he yelled. "Get on the phone, people. Find out everything you can. And someone get the story online!"

He rushed to a whiteboard on the wall and rewrote the top-five list of stories for the week. He put this at number one in big letters and brainstormed spin-offs to be printed in the rest of the paper and online.

The phone call to Lake was from somebody who lived near the army base. Lake rang him back for more information.

"I haven't got much more to tell you. I saw it from my house. It's the biggest explosion I've ever seen—bigger than fireworks."

"Any sign of casualties? Fatalities?"

"Lake, I don't know what to tell you. I can't tell from here, but it looks big."

"Any walls come down?"

"Yeah. There's bricks and stuff in the road. I can see that."

Lake leant back in his chair, caught the news editor's eye, and nodded as he asked the informant for more details. Mike hurried over to stand next to him so he could be updated.

Within minutes, several other phones were ringing with details from different contacts. No sooner had they put their handsets down than the phones rang again.

Within the next half hour, word about other events started coming in. It seemed there had been a series of explosions in and around Griffton. Buildings were on fire, including the central police station and a government building.

Eyewitness accounts came in thick and fast, and Mike quickly and expertly created an emergency response station. He had a team of journalists taking bystander reports by phone, several trawling the wires, one checking the main editorial inbox and Lake and another of the investigative journalists calling around to dig for more information.

At the same time, he wrestled with whether it was safe to send his team out across the city to have a look for themselves. There could be more carnage coming. For the time being, he felt responsible for their lives and was happy for the TV crews down the road to do that job.

Lake slipped in a call to his parents.

His mum answered. "Lake, are you all right?"

"Yes, I'm fine. I guess you've heard what happened?" Lake hunched over his computer, bowing low to the desk.

"I'm watching the news now. You should get out of the centre if you can. Lake, what's going on? I can't get hold of your dad."

Lake blanched. His dad's offices were near the government building that had been hit.

"I'll try him myself in a minute. Listen, I think I'm safe here, but I'll get home as soon as I can. I love you, Mum."

Lake sat up and looked around. The summer sun had set, and artificial light bleached the figures around him. The air in the newsroom was thick, and his colleagues looked grey and tired.

Lake was at the eye of a storm where the weightless ones floated. Though he couldn't see it from his window, he fancied he could feel the heat from the buildings burning across the city.

CHAPTER 8

The journalists at Griffton News did their best to nail down the facts by speaking to as many observers as possible. But people were hurting out there, lots of people, and it was tough work.

They found out that the emergency services had successfully closed off the army base, which was their highest priority because of its armoury. However, they were stretched thin in the other areas that had been attacked, and this put the public at risk. There were already a few reports of looters breaking into the burning buildings. Some of them had escaped with the spoils, while others had been injured or even killed by the heat, the smoke, and collapsing floors. The Griffton resident Lake spoke to showed signs of wear and tear, and he felt for them.

Nobody had claimed responsibility for the day's attacks, and there was a lot of gossip and confusion going on. Of course, people recalled the attack on the Griffton Metropolitan Hotel from the previous year. That had been a mindless and inexplicable act of violence carried out by a small group of terrorists with no apparent agenda. Many feared it was happening again.

For the people of Griffton, the spectre of the meaningless, motiveless attack chilled their blood. They had never fully understood why that strange cult had targeted the hotel in the first place. It had remained a mystery, affecting the psyche of the city.

In the end, after a long evening in the office, the News Editor called it a day. They had completed today's stories and put the paper 'to bed' so it could be printed during the night, ready for delivery in the morning.

"Can I have your attention? Quiet down over there. Go home, everybody except my core team—you know who you are. It looks like local TV is on top of the stories. Go home. Check on your families. Keep your TVs on and come in early. We pick up in the morning."

"You going home?" Lake asked Harvey.

His friend had lost his swagger and was ashen-faced. "I guess so. My folks are out east. There's no one at home at my apartment. Just the cat. Anyone going for a drink?"

The other reporters shook their heads. "How about you, Mike," asked Lake.

"Me? I'm staying here. But you guys should get out of here. Off you go."

LAKE CHECKED in with his mum again, who had finally located his father, Blake. He was on his way home.

Back at the house, they hugged each other, and his mother cried while his dad looked grim. He had loosened his red tie and opened two buttons on his shirt. He had the aroma of stale sweat and the vestiges of panic.

It had been a near miss for him, as the insurance firm where he worked was near the government building that had been bombed. They had been forbidden from leaving the building for extended hours until all was safe, and it had put a heavy burden on the office coffee machine.

"I was in a meeting when it happened. The entire office

shook. I thought it was an earthquake or something," said Blake, sitting at the kitchen table with an empty glass in front of him. He added, "But Andy – Andy Cooper – thinks he actually saw one of the people who attacked the building."

He had Lake's attention.

"It sounded pretty crazy when he told us, but he said it looked like the man was wearing strange, mediaeval armour, like those people who dress up at weekends and enact famous battles – or Vikings. I mean, he could have been mistaken."

"Did he tell the police?" asked Anne.

"We tried to ring but couldn't get through."

"The police station was attacked as well," said Lake.

"Maybe they'll bring in reinforcements from out of town?"

"Let's hope so," Lake answered.

"It's late now. Why don't we try to get some sleep?" Anne urged them.

"No. You go up if you want, my dear. I want to follow it on TV for a bit. See if they get any answers," said her husband.

"I've had enough for one day," said Lake, heading for his room.

"I love you, kid," said Blake.

Lake smiled wearily and went up.

HE SLEPT BADLY THAT NIGHT, eager to get back into the office and learn more about the attacks.

At one point in the night, after finally falling asleep, Lake woke with a start and turned on the bedside light. He was momentarily startled by his surroundings; novels and newspapers on the floor, messy shelves, and discarded clothing. In that instant, he was lying in a war-torn building, gutted by an explosion. His body was cut and bloody, lacerated by broken glass.

Then he slid back into reality and recognised his own home and his rollerblades and pads in the corner. Yesterday's incident had burned itself into his unconscious mind, just like his imprisonment last year. It was part of him now, and nothing was going to remove the stain.

Through the night and into the morning, the idea of contacting Rachel gnawed at his mind, but he couldn't think of a good pretext to talk to her. They were no longer together, so why would she be interested in his well-being, his family, or anything he had to say?

Instead, he waited until a reasonable hour and texted Kumiko. Naturally, she didn't reply. He scolded himself for expecting her to come back to him instantly and for wasting half an hour looking at his watch. The aching hole inside him yawned again, reminding him he was empty and alone.

He showered and dried, picked his trousers up off his bedroom floor, chose some underwear and a clean shirt from the drawer, and got dressed. All of this he did in a daze, with the television on in the corner of his bedroom.

The TV news didn't provide any answers, though, and the repetitive cycle of stories started to irritate him. The coverage raised more questions than answers, and this only strengthened his resolve to get to the office and start phoning around.

By the time he got downstairs, his father had already left for work, and his mum gave him a lingering hug and said, "Be careful out there?"

"I will, Mum. Anyway, somebody has to write today's news." He smiled a cheeky smile, and she ruffled his hair just as she always did. It made him feel like a toddler.

"Oh, Mum."

As soon as Lake left the house, he sensed that the atmosphere in Griffton was different. People in the street were smiling wearily at each other and tentatively making eye contact. This was something they rarely did, except for national events like royal weddings or big sporting celebrations.

The sun had risen again, the sky was blue, and morning had come, but still, things seemed different: the volume of the city had been turned down low. Perhaps people were avoiding work today. Seagulls kept their distance and seemed muted, and the traffic rolled slowly down Roasting Vale Lane instead of thundering along.

He didn't see any carnage on his way to work. The buildings that had been hit were further north and not on his route. But it didn't stop him from looking at every tall building, scrutinising them for signs of damage. The grey-blue glass towers shot upwards overhead.

All the way into the Griffton News, he observed strangers continue to talk to each other and smile sadly. He frequently heard, "I know," and "yes, such a shame."

When he got in, he quickly assessed from the others there had been no significant news since last night. Instead, Griffton was coming to terms with being the victim of a horrific act of violence by an unknown group of criminals.

It was his job to find out who the perpetrators were. He needed to go to the 'Ground Zero' of one of the attacks and see for himself.

⁌ 12345 ⁊

MIKE WRIGHT LOOKED like a man who had stumbled from one nightclub to another and eventually passed out on the pavement. In reality, he'd just snatched a couple of hours of sleep under his desk in the middle of a night of non-stop news-watching. He wore a checked shirt, the same one from yesterday, and pale chinos, both heavily creased, and he smelled like last week. His greying hair tufted upwards in places, and his eyes were red.

"Hi, Mike. You know they have showers downstairs, don't you?"

"Very funny. I'll have one later. Coffee first. Let's wait another ten minutes for the stragglers to arrive, then get together for a news meeting in the back room." He gave Lake a tired smile, activating the wrinkles around his eyes.

"Get your thinking cap on for angles, boy."

Lake homed in on his desk, logged in, and raised both eyebrows at the number of new emails he had received overnight. His voicemail had also been under attack, with more messages than he got on a healthy news day.

As he listened, he played with the objects on his desk. Various companies sent in executive toys and branded office stationery across the past year. He was particularly fond of his wooden jigsaw pen holder and his tiny Newton's cradle. He loved free stuff; it was another great thing about being a journalist.

One day, a local doughnut company sent two massive boxes of fresh doughnuts, jam ones, iced ones, custard ones, and novelty ones, instantly making friends with the entire editorial department. Of course, in return, they got their coverage for the refurbishment and relaunch of their three stores across the city.

He scrawled some notes on a pad in shorthand and took off for the meeting in the back room.

The team was already assembled, with around a dozen writers and reporters of all shapes and sizes. They included a petite young woman, Monica, with straight blonde hair and bright eyes; Harvey, tall, young, and confident with a wiry crop of short black hair and an easy smile; and Don, with black-rimmed glasses, a sardonic smile, and a quick glance.

They were mainly young people, as teens and twenties were cheaper to hire and easier to boss around, but there were also a couple of seasoned hacks who lent weight to the team. Don was one of these.

Lake stood at the back, near the door, behind a row of seated reporters. Mike was holding court, listening to questions, and hearing the different angles. As they hit each of the major categories of who, why, what, where, when, and how, the editor leaned heavily over his jotter and scribbled notes, nodding, challenging, then assigning stories to each of the people around the table.

"Monica, you keep pressing the police force's media relations. See if we can get a clear number on the injured and the dead. See how it's going to affect policing today and if we should be worried, which is my guess. Harvey, you go for your angle on the military base, as it seems they're not letting anyone near. Don, yes, I like your thinking, but make some calls first and test the waters. Use your contact. He always comes up with something interesting."

He kept a few of them on the stories they were pursuing yesterday, but it was clear the attacks would be stories one, two, three, and four, with follow-up articles on the inside pages.

"I want to be one of the people who goes out this morning. I want to see it for myself and chat with real people face-to-face. I need to look people in the eye and feel what they're feeling," said Lake.

"Fine. But if that's the case, I want at least three stories from you by day's end in return. Why don't you go and check out the government building that got hit on the north side of town? Then check out the police station. Find out anything you can. Try to find people who were there yesterday evening. Get some good quotes. But no heroics."

"Who me?"

Mike fixed him with a wry smile.

"Before you go, everyone, I want to give you some food for thought."

"What do you mean?" asked Hayley, who covered media, entertainment, and restaurants for the paper.

Mike reached down under his seat and brought out a big, white plate that was covered by a massive paper napkin. As he brought it up to the table, he whipped it off with the flair of a magician, revealing a huge chocolate sponge cake cut into thick slabs.

"It happens to be my birthday today, but please, no 'Happy Birthdays.' I don't want anyone making a thing of it. There are people dead today who were breathing yesterday. We're the ones fortunate enough to be alive. I am happy to be alive, as happy as I get, anyway. So grab some cake, get to work, and remember we are delivering news today to a city mourning. Never forget that."

Mike sat back in his chair and gave everyone a glum smile. Quietly, they reached for their slice of cake. Mike had also brought out a pile of napkins, impressing Lake with his attention to detail.

"Okay. Everybody happy? In that case, I'm going to go down for a well-deserved shower. Stop sniggering, Harvey."

He sighed heavily, putting both hands on the table to lever himself up to standing. Just then, his cell phone started to vibrate. It was next to his jotter on the meeting room table. A split second later, Don's mobile phone went off.

Out in the main office, they could hear the chorus of unattended phones ringing, one after another, before each moved to voicemail.

Mike answered his phone, mouthed the word "go" to his team, and soon found he was standing in an empty meeting room. He listened intently to the caller, his gaze fixed blankly on the glass divider that separated him from the bustling newsroom.

CHAPTER 9

Lake was not fully prepared for what he was about to see or smell. As he walked onto the scene at City Square, the municipal quarter of the city, the phrase that came to mind was 'post-apocalyptic.'

The stench hit him first. It was the thick reek of burning rubber, charred wood, and smouldering masonry. The smell filled the square and made his stomach lurch as he gawped at the gutted shell that was once the central government building for taxation, benefits, and finance-related affairs. Hollywood had moved into town, and they were in charge of special effects, by the look of it. The only problem was that this was real.

Fractured brickwork and shattered glass rested, like a murky pool, around the remains of the offices as clusters of firefighters and rescue workers stood in a daze. They were weary from a chaotic night through which they had worked to quell the flames and locate survivors. They stared at Lake through haunted eyes, their charcoal faces and uniforms telling the story of long, desperate hours of pawing through the rubble.

The buildings on either side of the ruin had also been damaged by the blast. They displayed their guts to the morning light: a multicoloured patchwork of computer wiring, office furniture, and charred stationery.

Plastic gutters and fascia had buckled from the heat, dripping down the side of the building like a set of Dali clocks. Like an eyeless skull, the adjoining buildings stared blindly, one of them missing its roof, a blackened husk all that remained.

The other had an absent section of wall, and its windows had blown out. Office debris could be seen from the outside, with the frame of an ergonomic chair teetering on a pile of rubble. Down on the ground, the side of a nearby web booth had been sheared off.

After taking some time to adjust, Lake snapped into automatic and whipped out his notepad and pen. It was time to start documenting what he saw and talking to people. Readers would demand to know.

The rescue workers didn't want to be bothered, and neither did the firefighters, but he found a man who might talk. He was in his late eighties, sitting on the curb and gazing at the wreck of the structure. He had blackened hands that were cut in places, as were his arms, but he seemed keen to talk as Lake made his approach and introduced himself.

"Lake Emerson? From the newspaper, right? You're the guy who got kidnapped last year. I read your stories. I'll tell you what I know. It's just terrible. I live over there, above the tailors on Newton Street, just off the square. I'm Ernie Cooper."

"Can you tell me what happened, in your own words, Ernie?"

"They don't know what caused it, but I was in my apartment yesterday afternoon. The blast shook the whole square. I heard a loud boom. It blew out the windows and made the ceilings collapse – look!"

"It must have been quite an explosion," said Lake.

"I used to go there to check on my housing and pension payments. The girl who worked there was so kind to me. She had curly red hair and this sweet smile. Her name was Lucy, I think, or Lisa. I really hope she got out before…"

He stared at the building for a while, then began to sob quietly. Lake was just about to thank the man and move on when another figure approached—dressed in striped pyjamas and a dressing gown. The newcomer placed his hand on the seated man's shoulder. He was still wearing his slippers, and nobody seemed to notice or care. Like his friend, he was unshaven, with a serious, weary expression on his face.

"It's okay, Ernie. Let me take over. Lake Emerson, a pleasure to meet you. I was listening to your conversation. I live along the way from Ernie. He's my friend. I was also in my apartment—we live on Newton Street as well."

"Okay," said Lake, making notes.

"Dannie Ward. That's my name. You can quote me if you like. At first, I thought a plane had crashed into the building. Lena, my wife, thought it was an earthquake. We heard screaming. Then we came down and walked over to the square. The building was on fire. Everything was on fire. The floors had collapsed. Big clouds of dust there were. People running in all directions. My wife started screaming herself."

Lake nodded in encouragement, his face grave. "We tried to call the police. Everyone did. But they'd been hit, too. The fire brigade came quickly, which was good. They started putting the fire out. People were talking about it being a bombing, like last year. But you know all about that. I don't know what to think. It was a sound like I'd never heard before. It was so loud, Ernie here says it was like in the war."

"Do you know how many survivors there are? Or casualties?"

"I told the TV crew all I know. I think they said there were fifty or sixty people taken to Griffton General. Maybe more. They pulled some of them out of the rubble, but they're not doing so well. Not sure how many people didn't make it. They're still looking."

"Are you two going to be okay? Is your wife around?"

"Yeah, we're going to be okay. Lena's having a lie down. It's been a long night, but we've got electricity in the apartment."

Lake left the men and walked parallel to the front of the government building, glancing at the heaps of grey rubble and still trying to engage with the firefighters from time to time, who shook their heads or waved him away. Nobody wanted to talk.

Lake carried on. He could hear the birds singing, which was out of place, and the laughter of a toddler who was rapidly hushed by a grown-up. Griffton was in shock.

He became aware that somebody was following him at a distance, a scrawny girl about the same age as Lake, with dark-ringed eyes and a mop of strawberry blonde hair. Lake wandered over to the centre of City Square, a grassy area with wooden benches around a sundial. Shards of glass had been hurled out in the explosion. He stood on the grass around the sundial, remembering, randomly, that Lewis Caroll called it a 'wabe' in Jabberwocky. His fingertips touched the slender metal gnomon that pointed to the sky. It was cool beneath his fingers. He felt the presence of the girl behind him.

"Can I help?" he asked, turning slowly to her so as not to frighten her away.

She spoke to him through her hair. "I was here when it happened. Sitting here, on this bench," she walked over and laid her hand on one of the bench arms as though to prove it. Then, she sat down. She had a lisp and a slow way of speaking, and her eyes were round and expressive.

"But no one can know. I wasn't meant to be here, you see."

"Okay. So what's your name? I'm Lake." He sat down beside her with his notepad on his knee.

"I know who you are. You're the news guy, the one who wrote about that hotel last summer: about it getting blown up. I read all your stuff."

"Yes, that's me. So, what did you say your name was?"

"I didn't." She sat and stared across at the bombed-out building.

"So, what did you see?"

"Lots of people had gone home. I suppose it was a good thing. But there were still people working late in there. The square was empty. I was the only one."

Then, she fixed him with a steady gaze. "I think I saw them, the ones who did it. They went in, but they never came out."

"What did they look like?"

"There were two of them, wearing hoodies. Dark blue Gap hoodies and carrying big black bags. Gym bags."

"Anything else?" Lake was scribbling down notes, but the girl seemed indifferent to them.

"I didn't see their faces, but one of them was really tall. The other one was big and bulky. Like a bodybuilder, maybe."

"How do you know they were the ones who did it?"

"I saw them go in and go up to the front desk. And then I saw it happen." She glazed over, tears in her eyes. Lake nodded and waited.

"I've been thinking about it all night. It's hard to describe and hard to get your head around. My brother put a DVD and a couple of eggs in a microwave once, just for fun, and turned it up to full power. It kind of went weird colours and blew up."

"Was it like that?" asked Lake

"Not really. But it was a bit like that."

"What happened next?"

The girl said quietly, "After they let off their bombs, it all kind of caved in, the building, I mean. I saw big dust clouds. But to be honest with you, I got up and ran at that point. Like I said, I wasn't meant to be here."

"Thank you for telling me what you did. Have you told the police?"

"The police? Haven't you heard? They're all gone."

"I have heard that. But surely you must have seen some officers around?"

"No, they're all gone. Things are different now. Everything's different now."

THE GIRL WAS RIGHT; the police were gone. They seemed to have disappeared from the city overnight. Not just the main police headquarters but also the smaller branches in Polcombe and Sandy Bottom Cove. They just weren't around. Lake felt like he was living in a disaster movie.

A number of them had been killed during the police station attack; that much was clear, but it was now becoming apparent that the other officers could not be located. There were scores of them missing. It was almost as though they had been abducted by aliens or vaporised in their beds, thought Lake.

A quick call to the news desk confirmed that even the Chief of Police hadn't turned up to work. Nobody could get hold of him or his deputies. The entire chain of command had dissolved in an instant, leaving the Police's press relations in turmoil, according to Lake's colleague Monica. They just didn't have any answers for her.

HE PAID a visit to the ruins of the police station on the north side of town, a wide and squat building. It had been hit hard and completely razed to the ground. Once again, the stench of burning filled his nostrils.

He saw patches of strawberry-colored blood staining the black and grey heaps of twisted building materials, with smoke still wafting up from the ash. This time, the desolation was harder to bear, and Lake had to steel himself to capture his standard three sets of quotes from the onlookers. Each word felt heavier, the scene weighing on his spirit.

Several people had seen the attack this time, and when they spoke, their comments were weary and bleak.

"I saw the men go in. They looked like the sort of men who

usually get nicked. They were wearing hoodies, like those Zodiacs, you know," said one old woman. Lake raised an eyebrow.

Another sombre young woman confirmed, "I work over there, in that bakery. I heard a loud noise, like a boom and a crunch. Then lots of shouting and cries. I felt the shock wave from the blast shake the shop."

Lake made notes for his story, and she continued speaking. "You can see how it knocked out the windows along our row. I ran outside as quickly as I could and saw it all falling down, like a pack of cards." The quotes were gold dust for Lake, but it was grim work taking them down.

"Basically, it was just rubble on fire in the end. And now it looks like this. I didn't know anyone there, but she did, over there. She's the wife of one of the duty officers who was in there yesterday evening."

Lake turned to look at the officer's wife, who was standing at the side of the blasted building. She seemed lost in thought, staring into the cavernous depths of the police station, whose insides had been ripped open for the world to see.

Lake's heart felt like it was swelling to dangerous proportions and would choke him if he didn't leave the scene.

❧ 12345 ☙

Back at the office, Lake kept his sanity by getting words down on the page. He was fortunate enough to be writing the front- page news story and a big article on page two, continuing the story. One of the other reporters had been assigned to feed him facts and figures, but it was his interviews that would form the basis of the article, and he would get the main by-line.

He got his head down and started to weave the quotes together and shape the story, writing the first draft of the introductory paragraph.

All around him, writers got to work, assembling the news

and analysis that would tell the people of Griffton the story of the attacks and the whys and wherefores.

Then it came: the tragedy of names. Web reports and phone calls flooded the news offices with the names of the dead, each name signifying a mother, a father, a brother, a grandparent, a spouse, or a friend. Frequent contact with the hospital made the list longer with each call.

Mike Wright started to put together a special section honouring those who had lost their lives since yesterday. In total, there were ninety-three dead and two hundred and six injured: Griffton's greatest tragedy. That night, a candlelight vigil was going to be held in a secondary school, open to the public. Some Griffton News readers were nervous about attending it, feeling the vigil itself could be a target for the attackers. Others were defiant. They needed an outlet to express their anger, fear, and grief.

There was still no clear reason Griffton had been hit in such a swift and ruthless way. Nobody had claimed responsibility, and although the attacks seemed to be on military or policing installations, people considered the bombing of the government building to be beyond the pale.

"No one likes paying their taxes," said Harvey. "But you don't go and put a bomb under the building that collects them. Roads, schools, and hospitals have to be built. A lot of ordinary people worked there—housing officers, you know? I just don't get it."

"Neither do I," said Lake.

Mike Wright came over to the central hub and said, "Attention, everybody. Eyes on the screen right now."

A room full of eyes turned to the big plasma screen on the wall next to Mike's whiteboard.

Live images were coming through from other cities: Manchester, Birmingham, London, and Bristol. It wasn't just Griffton; buildings were burning across the land. The country was in flames.

CHAPTER 10

Lake finally got hold of Kumi and pressed her to have a coffee with him. They met at Vinod's Coffee Pot, a short walk from the Griffton News tower. It was another day of the city being strangely serene, as though people were treading carefully, speaking softly, and even driving their cars more quietly.

It was late afternoon, coming up to the time the attacks had occurred the previous day. They got a table by the window so they could watch the people going by. Both of them were inveterate people watchers.

Kumi seemed distracted. Although she sat with the usual poise, she fiddled with her handbag and then her sugar packets.

"Did you get my texts?" he asked.

"I have a lot of work on," she answered frostily. She checked her reflection in the eyes of a couple of men who passed by the table.

"So, tell me, what is it you actually do?"

"I'm involved in logistics and planning. The organisation's global, but they also have local offices."

"Do you enjoy it?"

"Yeah – it's okay. A lot of fun, really. The travel's great. I've always liked travelling." She sounded bored, looking just past Lake's shoulder as she spoke. Then she stared into her macchiato for several minutes.

"When did you leave Griffton?"

"What do you mean?"

"You know, when you were little?"

"Oh. Yeah, I was a little girl, and my parents took the family abroad to Oz."

"Remind me, how is it you know Rachel?" Lake asked in a neutral tone.

"You don't really want to talk about her, do you? You're here with me."

"No, you're right," he sighed. "So, how are things going?"

"Things?" Kumi looked him in the face. "Things are on track. How about you?"

"It's been a tough morning, to be honest. I've seen some things today that I thought I'd never see. I saw a war zone today. You know those attacks?"

"Of course, I know about them," she snapped.

"Yup. Well, I have to cover them for the paper. I went to the places, City Square and the Police HQ. I've done some tough stories before, but this was definitely the hardest. It seems like…"

"Lake, shut up, will ya? Let's talk about something else. There's too much of it in the news at the moment, wouldn't you agree?"

"I suppose so, yeah. So, I guess it would be insensitive to ask if you'd like to catch a movie later?"

"You've got that right, cowboy."

"Yeah, yeah. Griffton's hurting. It wouldn't be right. Some other time then?"

Kumi said nothing; she just watched people over Lake's shoulder, her eyes like giant, sideways raindrops defined by black eyeliner. The space between the two of them grew wider.

"Listen, Lake, I have things to do now. I'll see you around."

"Aren't you going to finish your coffee?"

"See you later, mate."

With the swish of a leather coat and a cloud of perfume, Kumi was gone.

12345

LAKE GOT a phone call that afternoon from Robbie the Zodiac.

"How did you get this number?"

"The paper gave it to me."

"I see." Lake started to sweat. It was a fortnight since he had become part of the Zodiac pack. He had wormed his way into the gang of youths in order to research them for a news story. It had taken all of his charm to get their trust and learn what he could.

But having been discovered as the news reporter he was, he knew it was just a matter of time before they found him and exacted some terrible revenge for betraying them. In fact, he thought about it frequently. It wouldn't take much for one of them to follow him to work one day and make him disappear.

"It was just business, you have to understand. I was doing my job. All I wanted to do was write about you guys, not get you into any trouble," he pleaded.

"Don't worry about all that," said Robbie in his slow Scottish accent. "I didn't call to threaten you."

"What then?"

"I didn't know who else to call. They're all gone. Stevie chased them out of our warehouse after something bad happened last week. But I can't really talk about that. After everyone went, it was just me, Stevie, and Pig for a bit."

"Then what?"

"Then last night, Stevie and Pig never came home. We were meant to go down the beach today, doing the usual. But they never came back. I heard the news stories, Lake. They never told me about it, but could they have done it?"

Lake's mind raced ahead like an over-clocked processor. "There's something else as well. We were doing a job for this man, someone called Benson."

"Benson Steel?"

"Do you know him?"

"Yes, I've interviewed him. He's a businessman who owns properties across the city. He's a bit of a tough nut if you ask me. No one seems to like him."

"He's dead."

"Come again?"

"We did a job for him, and now he's dead. I don't understand any of it. They wanted us to break into a house."

"Okay, can you tell me more?"

"It was a big house near the cliff."

Lake bristled and pressed his phone tightly to his ear.

"I've got an idea. Let's meet up, you and me? This sounds really interesting. We could meet somewhere neutral, like a cafe. Not at the warehouse."

"Not me. I'm gone." Robbie hung up.

THE LOOTING STARTED that very night. With no police to restrain them and the citizens living in fear of another terrorist attack, ex-Zodiacs and wayward teenagers ransacked the malls and shopping arcades.

Mangled doorframes rested on the pavement with beads of glass lying like discarded teeth all around. Inside the stores, naked clothes rails stood like the skeletons of dead robots, with a carpet of merchandise covering the floor. Products were trampled underfoot, sending pottery, plastic, and glass shards everywhere.

With armfuls of colourful, branded trainers, mobile phones, and computer consoles, the young people sprinted in all directions.

Griffton Mall was flooded with underage gangsters, smirking and hollering, rampaging through their own neighbourhood, smashing and stealing as they danced. A tidal wave of destruction washed across the city, from the top to the bottom, not even sparing the waterfront shops.

A concrete boulder was thrown through the window of Rock and Shock, the record shop where Rachel and Iona worked. Film and music discs were snatched and scattered like cheap trinkets on the floor while law-abiding citizens kept their distance and watched from the shadows.

It was a night of freedom, a night of partying. The sounds of shouting, swearing, and joking could be heard right across town, contrasting the silence of the day.

Soon, the city thugs mingled with ordinary school kids and opportunistic adults, looking to raise their standard of living for free. Everybody took exactly what they wanted, revelling in the fact that it was there for the taking.

Soon, expensive watches, tailored suits, and even sports cars were liberated from their stores.

But it didn't stop there. Emboldened by the ease at which their prizes yielded themselves, a forward-thinking gang of youths broadened their strategy. Moving on from the shops, they targeted some of the town houses at the centre of the city. It made sense to them since everything was going free.

It was around midnight. For many people, robbing shops was clearly unacceptable, but it was the job of the police to stop them, and insurers would pay out in the end.

The citizens quickly changed their minds when their own houses came under fire. The mob turned up first at one house, then the next, moving its way down Newton Street. In response, a group of vigilante dads gathered, weapons in hand, and drove the youths out of their houses, one home at a time.

One father, transfigured with rage, wielded a pair of bolt cutters, his crazed expression lit by the moonlight. Another had a butcher's knife. People got beaten. Some died.

The stark white moon oversaw the pitched battle at the centre of Griffton. Cowering in a massive black sky, the moon watched as one huge, bear-like man whirled a pipe around his head. A teenage boy lay clutching his side, blood soaking his clothes. Others sprawled on the concrete, limbs stretched wide. Once again, buildings were burning in Griffton, heating the atmosphere.

Around three o'clock in the morning, Griffton prison was blown open near the west end of the Cliff. It was a strategic explosion, collapsing several walls and opening the building up like a cardboard box. Dazed by the attackers' audacity, the prison guards failed to stem the flow of prisoners who scrambled from the jail and ran down towards the city.

Paulo Kowalski sat at the foot of his grandfather's grave in Katowice, a city in southern Poland where he had lived since he was a baby. His grandfather had been a coal miner all his life, working at Wujek Coal Mine, just outside the city.

Wujek was opened way back in the Sixteenth Century and was known across Poland as the place where striking miners were massacred back in the early eighties. His grandfather had always been reluctant to talk about those dark days but had remained sombre and reflective ever since.

From where he sat, Paulo could see the skyscrapers that stood along Chorzowska, Korfantego, and Roździeńskiego Street in the centre of the city. His favourites were the newest office buildings, the A-class ones: Altus Skyscraper and Silesia Towers. These two towers were near the mall in the city centre and connected to it by an underground tunnel.

Paulo was reading a fat book by Dostoyevsky, something he was studying as part of his English college course. He was enjoying it quite a lot, although the language was difficult in some places. He persevered and gave it his best shot because he wanted to be an English teacher and work abroad, hopefully somewhere warmer. Poland could get freezing in the autumn and winter, and his heart longed for sunnier climes.

The book was about murder and motives, and the main character, Rodion Raskolnikov, was sometimes a hero and sometimes a villain, depending on how he argued away the murder he had committed. The essay that he had to write was about whether there was a difference between murder and killing, and it made his head hurt to think about it.

The book was helping, though, and he was getting an understanding of the whole issue of ending someone's life. Rather than making him feel morbid and unhappy, sitting next to his grandfather's grave was helping him. He knew it shouldn't be that way, but being close to his grandpa also gave him some peace.

As usual, his mind wandered away from the text, and he looked around him, then gazed into space in an unfocused way. A gigantic bird flew across the cold summer sky. He could see it was bulky and bulbous despite being far away. The sky was empty apart from the bird. Paulo turned back to his novel.

A few minutes later, he heard a thump in front of him. Staring at him through two beady eyes was a furry bird creature with a large body and long, black wings. It looked like a tough little thing, with the boldness of a domestic pet begging for food. It was sitting on the grass that covered his grandfather's grave, just in front of the tombstone.

"What kind of bird are you?" asked Paulo, wondering whether the creature was a bird at all. "Or are you a bat?"

The creature let out a strange cry, revealing a tiny pink tongue.

"Well, you are sitting on my grandfather's grave."

The creature stuck its furry head forward and gave a small hiss.

"I am the one who should be offended," Paulo laughed. "I don't have any food for you if that's what you are after," he added.

The creature backed away towards the gravestone and spread its wings to fly away. Paulo relaxed and went back to his book.

A split second later, the animal attacked him, leaping towards him with its mouth open. Its teeth were like sharp blades, ready for action.

Instinctively, Paulo snapped his book shut and brought it back to swat the creature with a forceful tennis-style swing. There was a sharp clunk as the book struck his attacker, hard board hitting bone.

But, taking mere seconds to recover, the beast was back on its feet. This time, it flew straight at him and struck its mark. Its teeth sank into Paulo's index finger, and he let out a yelp of pain as the beast clamped down with ferocious strength.

CHAPTER 11

Griffton was on a knife edge for the next ten days, with neighbourhoods banding together to keep watch and protect themselves. There hadn't been any more explosions since that first night, though the citizens were edgy.

In the police's absence, a civilian security force had emerged with its own hierarchy and rules. The Neighbourhood Watch groups fed into this structure, staying vigilant and monitoring their streets. Unlike the Neighbourhood Watch of old, which twitched lace curtains and tutted when a stranger walked down the road, the new regime fought crime where it could, catching burglars and hunting down criminals. It was run by the people, for the people, and was answerable to the majority.

The looters were still a problem, flaring up unexpectedly across the city to claim their prizes. At first, there seemed to be a distinction between honest citizens and those who wanted something for nothing. Common decency had a place for the moment, but the slide into moral decay was an ever-present threat. Groups of teenagers and twenty-somethings sneaked around, looking for easy targets. Meanwhile, vigilante gangs roamed the city, armed to the teeth, seeking the miscreants.

Revenge punishments were meted out daily, but they did not stop the looters from striking. The gains were too great, the winnings too appealing.

As one side took up their weapons, so did the other. Some teenagers found themselves swords and small handguns, knives, knuckledusters, and baseball bats. But so did the vigilantes. If a lone warrior from one side or the other was caught in a dark alley with insufficient weaponry, it would be the end for them.

Small-time gangsters and escaped convicts presented another level of peril. Isolated murders and arson attacks were reported right across Griffton, with no one able to predict or prevent them. Parts of the city quickly became no-go areas, but there were also gated communities that had more embedded security. Watchmen stood guard night and day alongside their attack dogs, Pit Bulls and Staffordshire Terriers, who growled at the shadows and bared their sharp teeth.

LAKE DID his best to travel safely from home to work and report on the events as they unfolded. He had also taken to carrying a knife after being confronted by muggers in the town centre. On that occasion, he gave up his phone and some cash but managed to get away with his life.

"If only I had the guts to carry a gun," he thought.

Lake heard some idiots had targeted the hospital and tried to run away with some drugs. It was yet another sign that Griffton was imploding without the police.

He heard similar things from other cities and towns across the nation. He wondered how long the situation could carry on as it was. The government held emergency meetings on a daily basis. Still, nobody seemed to have any wisdom about what to do from now on. The leaders were following the populace, and the people took matters into their own hands.

"Everything's on its head," Lake sighed.

The attempted robbery at the hospital prompted Lake to check on Iona, Rachel's friend. He learned she was recovering from the car accident at home. He remembered where she lived because he had met Rachel there on a couple of occasions. He had even been out socially with Iona and Rachel a few times over the past year.

She was friendly, if a little formal, when he turned up at her door, but this was to be expected. After all, he was no longer with Rachel, and she had probably poured out her heart to her friend behind his back. He would know quickly if his name was mud here.

The signs were good, though, and Iona invited him in. Soon, he sat on a stool at her kitchen breakfast bar. Her place was multi-coloured, something that immediately lifted Lake's spirits. She was hobbling along on crutches and told him breezily that she preferred to sit on a bar stool at the moment as she couldn't get down to the beanbags or low sofas in the front room.

She made some peppermint tea, seeming to be out of anything caffeinated. Lake took a sniff at it, finding it hot and surprisingly pleasant.

"So, you're not at work today?"

"No, my boss temporarily closed the shop. It got hit the other night by the looters." Iona's sunny demeanour slipped behind a cloud.

"Anyone hurt?"

"No, but they left Rock and Shock in quite a state. One broken window and disks all over the floor. It took Ben a while to clear up, and I couldn't exactly help with my leg in this state. We could have done with Rachel's help. Any idea what she's up to? She hasn't checked in at work for days now, and I can't get hold of her."

"That's funny."

"No, it isn't."

"No, I mean it's strange. Rachel and I split up. Did you know that?"

"No, I didn't. I'm sorry. But really? You two aren't together anymore?"

"She wrote me a note before she went up country. She dumped me by letter. I suppose it's one level better than being dumped by text or email."

"So, she's gone away? I didn't know that either! Ben could really have done with knowing that. However, he did have to close the shop, so finding a replacement for Rachel hasn't been top of his list. We did both wonder where she was, though. She didn't say anything at all about going away unless she didn't want to worry me because I was in the hospital. Still, she could have told me. She knows that."

"So, you didn't know? I thought you two were best friends."

"Well, you know Rachel. Sometimes, she talks. Sometimes she doesn't."

"Tell me about it. Anyway, she gave me this note before she left."

"You carry it around with you?"

"Yeah," Lake said sheepishly.

Iona read the note out loud. Meanwhile, Lake fidgeted.

"Dear Lake, I've taken some time off work, and I'm going away for a bit to stay with my family in Birmingham. Things aren't really working out between us, and, to be honest, there is no more 'you and me.' I know you know what I'm talking about. Anyway, I'd rather you didn't try to call me. But I'm sure I'll see you around. By the way, things went fine up at the house. There's nothing to worry about anymore, and it's all cool now. Well, take care. Rachel."

Iona stared at the letter and read it over again, to herself this time.

"So, you two have definitely split up? She never mentioned it. But then again, she did say you liked somebody else." Iona stared hard at Lake.

"Did she? Oh, you mean Kumiko? Oh no, there's really nothing between us."

"I see."

"No, Kumi's a friend from Rachel's childhood. They grew up together, and then Kumi was taken abroad with her family."

"Rachel never mentioned her to me. She didn't tell me she was going up to Birmingham either. I'm going to try calling her again."

Iona tried Rachel's mobile and left a message.

"It's me again. Lake's here, asking after you," she smiled at Lake. "He says you're up in Birmingham? Well, you really should have told Ben, or at least me. Give me a call."

She snapped her clamshell phone shut and brought out some little butter biscuits.

"No thanks, I should get back to work. Are you feeling better?"

"A bit. Ben says rest up, and there's no need to rush back to work. He's manning the store on his own, hoping to open up soon. How about you? How's the paper? I saw your story last week on the front page. It made me cry."

"You know us news reporters. We keep trooping on."

Iona scribbled something down on a rainbow Post-it notepad.

"Here's my number in case you hear from Rachel before I do."

"Cheers."

❧ 12345 ❧

THAT VERY AFTERNOON, the bombings started again. It was a series of bus bombs this time, taking Griffton by surprise. The brutality and apparent randomness of the attacks were shocking. Buildings have natural layers to protect people if they are attacked, but buses are just metal boxes when it comes down to it. They're all hard metal poles, metal panelling, upholstered seats, and soft human beings. Survivors were low.

The scenes were identical in City Square, on Griffton Boulevard, and Roasting Vale Lane, where the three bombs were detonated. In each location, the carcass of a burned-out bus sat smoking. There was a gaping hole where the detonation had ripped right through, leaving twisted metal, blackened seats, and charred bodies. Some witnesses ran screaming at the sight, panic gripping their hearts. Others stood transfixed, staring with their mouths open. All traffic halted.

No police arrived or any official help. The emergency services were late, or else they weren't coming at all. It was left to brave bystanders to pull survivors out of the metal cage and lay them on the pavements. It was another dark day for Griffton.

LAKE MET up with Kumi again. She surprised him by arriving on a huge black Kawasaki Ninja motorbike. It looked brand new, too.

She stared at him with her bike helmet under her arm, thick black eyeliner framing her eyes. She was wearing a biker's jacket over figure-hugging leathers, and her hair was tangled from wearing the helmet. Lake caught his breath.

After a long while, Kumiko said, "You've got to quit bugging me, mate. All the texts and the voicemails. Enough!"

It was evening, and they were standing outside Klub Kafka, a nightclub and bar at the end of one of Griffton's beach-side lanes. Kumi left Lake standing and walked to the entrance of the bar, an ultramodern affair with white furnishings and fittings and ambient lighting. A security guard stopped her at the door and checked her photo ID.

"You look a little young, miss," commented the man at the door.

Kumi growled at him, "Yeah, I know. It's a curse. Check the date of birth."

He squinted at the driver's licence and pulled a face as she waited. Lake shuffled his feet.

"Okay, go on through."

Since the attacks, all of the city's bars had beefed up security, installing metal window protection and hiring a double layer of guards.

Lake followed Kumi, flashing his ID and press badge. The chunky security guard gave him a menacing look but, after a moment of hesitation, allowed him inside.

The atmosphere inside Klub Kafka was relaxed, which was a refreshing change. Over the last two weeks, Lake noted the citizens had become increasingly edgy and reluctant to talk. Even his most talkative contacts had gone silent, not wanting to draw attention to themselves.

Lake bought two drinks and joined Kumi at the table she'd chosen in one of the corners. Klub Kafka used to have a band on every night, and a late-night drinks licence, but Lake learned from the barman that everything had been scaled back for security reasons. The venue was now closed at eleven, and there were only a couple of bands willing to play.

Over on the side, people relaxed with their drinks, taking turns to try out a new immersive virtual video game.

Kumi shrugged off her jacket and played with the candle holder at the centre of the table.

"So, how have you been?"

"Busy. Out of town and up country. Lots going on."

"Remind me, what is it you do?"

She stared past his left shoulder and said in a bored voice, "Logistics, project management, change management, that sort of thing."

"Have you got any interesting projects on at the moment?"

"Yeah, a few. You?"

Then Lake exploded, "Look, Kumiko. We've been seeing

each other for two weeks now. Granted, Griffton's gone crazy, and the world is about to end, but I thought you liked me. Are you even reading my texts? I've told you how I feel about you. Why won't you say how you feel about me? It's like I have to do all the work, you know?"

She sat back and smiled a thin smile.

"You don't give much away, do you?" he added.

"I've been like this for a long time. That's the way I like it."

"He must have really hurt you."

Lake tried to read her expression and failed. It might have been a condescending sneer.

"Do you even like me?" he asked desperately.

"I'm here, aren't I?" she snapped.

Lake knew instinctively that he had committed relationship suicide by acting like a complete idiot.

He sighed and let his cold beer slide down his throat. All around him, contented people chatted with each other. Everyone else seemed happy and relaxed. He, on the other hand, felt like a small child who had wandered downstairs and blundered into the grown-ups' party.

Then it struck him. Kumi didn't really like him, not in that way. Okay, perhaps she thought he was cute. But it was clear that he was getting too heavy for her. If only he could be more chilled out about life.

He looked across the table at her and realised in an instant that she wasn't Rachel. There was a Rachel-sized hole in his heart, which only Rachel Race could fill.

Kumi was wearing a stern expression. At last, she spoke in a husky voice, fixing him with her cold eyes. "Look, Lake, I'm not sure, okay? I'm still sussing you out. How do I feel? Well, I really don't know."

Lake leant back and sighed.

A band arrived on the stage at the far side of Klub Kafka. They were shambolic but cocky, dressed in black t-shirts and drainpipe jeans. The guitarist strummed through a few chords, scowling through a long fringe of brown hair, and the lead singer stepped up to the microphone. He was unshaven, had terrible acne, and had a croaky voice.

"Ladies and gentlemen. We are Social Vomit."

"No kidding," said Kumi. "Hey, Lake, I've got to go back to work."

"Right now? At night? You're working at night?"

"Enjoy the band," she said quietly, picked up her black crash helmet, and crept out of the bar.

CHAPTER 12

"Oh, this is good. This is very good. Excellent, in fact. The city is ours," said Samyaza in the dreamy tones of his surfer boy avatar. Kumi smiled. She was back in Daniel's study.

"Tell me one thing, Sammy. If you're doing this all over the country, all over the world, then what's so special about Griffton?"

"Have you heard of the phrase 'think globally, act locally'? That's what I enjoy doing. I like winning people over one by one, one heart, one soul at a time. Of course, I want the whole world for us, and I want the world to know me and follow me. But the way I do things is to win them one by one. It's the way I've always worked. As you told the reporter boy, I've been like this for a long time. That's the way I like it."

"You heard me say that?"

"I hear everything."

"So, did you like that line? It's yours for free if you want it."

"Why, thank you. And here's a line for you: everything is about to change. Everything you know, everything the people of Griffton know, everything that is familiar, it's all about to change."

"It's already changed so much," said Kumi excitedly.

"You ain't seen nothing yet, girl."

"There's more?"

"Oh yes, so much more. Next up is your TV debut. You're going to enjoy this one. Just smile and look pretty, and I'll help you say the right things. It will be a piece of cake."

"Sounds like fun. I've always wanted to be on TV."

"Well, now's the time. Why don't you go and get yourself a drink and some food, and I'll fill you in on the details?"

"I think I will," Kumi responded. She stared into the fire, watching the blue-tipped flames jump around. She inhaled the heady aroma of burning wood.

Then she got up and went to the kitchen, passing half a dozen Dream Fighters on the way.

"I hope you guys left some food for me," she snapped.

THAT WEEK, chaos prevailed in the streets of Griffton. Along with the looting and vandalism came a more sinister occurrence. There were reports of incidents where houses had been attacked and individuals taken in the night. It even happened on the same road on which Lake and his family lived.

He heard breaking glass, which was not unusual in these dark days. It was several doors down, and although his father, Blake, had made tentative investigations, nothing seemed amiss until the morning.

Then, the horrific rumour went from house to house that a man had been kidnapped, a city lawyer who was helping to lead the local Neighbourhood Watch. Everyone in the street was shaken by the news, aware that the terrorism level had crept up even further.

"We have to do something," said Anne, with more than a hint of panic in her voice. She had gathered the neighbours in their front room and was dishing out cups of tea. Fifteen people were staring with their mouths open. Some people sobbed, while others sat silently and gazed into space. One old man paced around, blinking violently and shaking his head.

Somebody put an arm around Julia, the lawyer's wife, and she cried again. They had all searched their houses and gardens and asked friends, family, and anyone they could think of if they'd seen the man, Andy Schneider. But without a functioning police service, it was hard to get answers. People were left to their own devices, and mysteries abounded. Lake called into the paper and quickly found that other people had gone missing, too. It was too early for the News Editor, Mike Wright, to be in yet, but the editorial assistant, Gabrielle, seemed to be abreast of the situation.

She had heard from a few of the reporters, who made it their job to be the first into the office in the mornings, that other people were missing.

"It sounds like important people all over the city have been captured. Harvey thinks some of the Neighbourhood Watch leaders have gone. So far, no one's seen anyone being taken. All we know is that loads of people are missing."

"Thanks, Gabrielle. You look after yourself and tell Harvey and the rest that I'm coming in right now."

Lake's stomach lurched, and he felt prickles across his face.

It felt to him like the sea had swept up onto the beach, claimed a shell here, a pebble there, and a stranded starfish over there, and clawed them back into the deep. It left no trace beyond an empty bed or chair.

These terrorists, the same ones who were blowing up buildings, were waging some sort of psychological warfare against the city and, in fact, the entire country. Nobody knew who they were or what they wanted. If it was terror that they were trying to achieve, then they'd smashed their aim.

Unable to be of any further use to the neighbours, Lake went back to work.

Once in, he quickly learned from Harvey that there was no

sign of the News Editor. Mike was generally in by eight, well before the others. There was no answer on his mobile phone and no sign that he would be late. It was completely out of character.

Lake and Harvey stared at each other.

IN MIKE'S ABSENCE, Don took charge, being second in command. He wore a dark blue linen suit that was slightly crumpled and conducted himself in a sombre manner. Don held a news meeting in his usual hushed tones, looking hard at people over his black-rimmed glasses. Story number one was the disappearances.

Don wanted names, locations, details, and any available eyewitness reports. Several investigative journalists were assigned to work the angles of why people had been taken and where they had been taken. That is, if indeed they were still alive. Nobody mentioned Mike, but he was implied in every conversation and every nuance. They had an urgent and vested interest in finding him and solving the terrorists' latest riddle.

That afternoon, Lake got a phone call from Kumiko.

"Lake, it's me. I can't tell you much, but what I can tell you is that I know about some of the things that have been happening."

"You do? What do you know?"

"Shut up and listen a moment, you idiot. I like you, Lake. That's why I'm calling you. But you need to know that everything is about to change. Everything you know, everything the people of Griffton know, everything they take for granted, it's all about to change."

"What do you mean? How are they going to change? Do you know about the people who've disappeared?"

"All I can tell you is that things are going to change around here, and they're going to change very fast. You need to stick with me. I know people. People who can help us."

"Are you something to do with the attacks? Tell me, Kumiko. Tell me now. I need to know."

"Can you meet me? Outside Klub Kafka in three hours?"

"I can't be a part of this, Kumi. If you have anything to do with it, you need to get out. Get out as soon as you can."

"You don't understand, Lake."

"I think I understand perfectly."

"No, you don't. This thing is bigger than you and me. What's happening in Griffton is happening all around the world. We have people in place who can help with what's going on. They can take charge of the situation, Lake. You must join us."

"I can't believe this."

"Klub Kafka in three hours. Don't be an idiot. Meet me." She hung up.

Lake stared at his phone, his heart pounding. "No. I'm not going to meet you this time, ice queen," he muttered under his breath.

Shortly after, Don drew everyone's attention to the television screen. Staring at the carpet, deep in thought, he walked over and turned up the volume. All eyes were turned towards the flat screen. Somebody was about to come on who claimed they had information about the attacks and disappearances. The national news presenter chatted, speculated, and generally wasted time, and eventually, they brought on their guest.

It was Kumiko. The first thing Lake noticed was her big round spectacles that made her eyes look large and serious. She was wearing a sleeveless, olive-coloured linen dress, and her hair was tied back.

Her interview began. "We know who is attacking us, and we have proof. My organisation has been tracking them since before the attacks…"

"My organisation?" Lake exploded. He was quickly shushed from all sides.

Kumi carried on, "…when we knew they were highly organised and extremely dangerous. Now we know for sure." She spoke with an other-worldly confidence.

"Who exactly are they?"

Kumiko stared at the interviewer and stated, "They are a group of deluded terrorists who call themselves Dunamis followers. They are also known as followers of the Rescuer, who is their leader. No one has seen the Rescuer, but these fanatics believe he is worth dying for."

"What do they want?" asked the presenter.

"They want to destroy us and everything we stand for. Make no mistake, we are under attack, people. The entire nation is under attack, and they will stop at nothing. I know what these people are like and what they are capable of. Do not underestimate them. They are cunning and ruthless. We must stand together."

"But why are they doing this?"

"It's some sort of twisted religion. We always knew religion was dangerous. That's why we stamped it out. That's why all holy books were burned and adherents removed. This is further proof that we needed it. Religion is responsible for all wars. As for these Dunamis followers, they are dangerous and will show no mercy. They are trying to rob us of our freedom. We must not let them."

"Is that why they're kidnapping people?"

"Their reasons for this are unknown. All I can tell you is that this is a war, and in wars, there are casualties."

"Why should we trust you and your people?" the presenter asked sternly.

Kumi was as solid as an iceberg. She looked into the camera and said without stuttering or blinking, "My organisation is ready to help. We are humanitarian, and we are humanistic, by which I mean we do not believe in the supernatural, like the cult members who are attacking us. No, we believe in the importance of human life. But we are calm and rational at all times, unlike the enemy. We are also fully prepared. We have a private army at hand, and we are at your disposal. We have bases across the country."

"And who is this army?"

Kumi smiled confidently at the question. "We have been in training for many months for such a time as this. Our Dream Fighters are ready to step in to stem the violence and protect the cities."

She continued, "The Dream Fighters are an elite troop of highly trained soldiers who love this great nation of ours and will defend it to the death. If any of you want to join our ranks, we are willing to train you. We have protective uniforms ready for you. We have plenty of weapons to defend ourselves. We are ready to fight back. The terrorism ends here."

"How soon can you help us?"

"We are ready right now. We can come to your aid right now if you want us to – London, Manchester, Birmingham, even Griffton. We are ready to help today. Today. But be warned, people. They are amongst us. These Dunamis followers are in our midst, and they could strike at any time. Be vigilant, be prepared, and come join us. We are the defenders of a way of life that is under attack, a life of freedom that we love dearly and cherish with all our hearts. No one will rip it away from us. No one."

CHAPTER 13

It was a place of mammoth rocks with spiny undergrowth poking out between them like fingers, reaching into the air. These large boulders lay between fields of green grass on one side and a sparse, dry valley on the other, which stretched ahead for miles.

Sandalphon, one of the Rescuer's warriors, picked his way carefully through the needles and placed his hand on one of the rocks to steady himself. They provided cover from the enemy and an excellent vantage point from which to survey the valley.

He stared out across the yawning wasteland. The sky cast a purple glow across the grey rocky floor, and the tall warrior angel scanned the horizon carefully, searching for hostile forces.

He noted the valley had very few features, a tree or two dotted here and there and some squat bushes. There were also small groups of stones or rocky indentations on the ground, but little that could be used for cover. The rugged plain stretched into the far distance in all directions, growing hazy to the far left and right as it met the mountains.

It looked clear enough. Sandalphon knew they had to cross the valley to get to the hinterlands, where they would join their master. The Rescuer had temporarily left his band of fighters for an undisclosed mission, and his followers knew it was not theirs to ask questions. He often had business of his own to attend to. Like the trusting servants they were, they were confident he would update them later if necessary.

They had immediately suffered from the absence of their leader, though. Shortly after his departure, the group was pounced on by a group of demonic spirits. These violent brutes lusted after their destruction. The beasts came upon them suddenly. They leapt from the branches of a nearby tree and hauled the riders off their horses.

The angels slew many, scattering the rest, but it put them on their guard for the rest of the day. The following hours were tense as they expected another attack, but none came.

Sandalphon turned to his comrade, Mattatron, and said, "It looks like the coast is clear. We should go back and tell the others. If we strike camp now, we could make it to that first clump of trees by nightfall. What do you think?"

"I agree. But I don't like being in the open without the King," said Mattatron.

"If we stick together, we'll be back with him before long. Let's tell the others."

They turned and started to walk back to the camp a couple of kilometres away.

No sooner had they passed the last boulder when Sandalphon and Mattatron found themselves locked in combat.

Four large Angel Hunters had emerged from behind the boulders. Their stench was overpowering. They rushed at the two with their fangs bared and a ferocity that took the angels by surprise.

Each of their attackers had a pair of leathery black wings hanging from their shoulders like a cloak. Their eyes flashed with hatred, and a sound came from deep in their throats: a cross between a hiss and a roar.

Sandalphon felt powerful arms around him and teeth trying

to sink into his neck. Bulbous flesh pressed against him, and he felt a sharp pain as a set of talons bit into his back.

He gagged as the demon brought its face close to him and stared poisonously through two jet-black eyes. Its irises and pupils were the colour of midnight on a moonless night.

Sandalphon wrestled vigorously, trying to break free. They tussled and twisted, two immortal beings who were both powerful fighters and skilled in close combat.

Meanwhile, Mattatron thrashed about with his short sword, swiping and stabbing expertly. It was an ancient blade that had seen much action. Each jagged nick told a story.

One creature fell to his blade, his side lacerated and his blood painting the rocks. Screeching in agony, he slumped to the ground, dead. His spirit passed out of the underworld with his final breath and raced back home to Earth.

Mattatron despatched a second nightmare spirit, sending him howling back to the Earth, leaving the dead shell of a monster body behind as its spirit was ejected from the mezzanine world.

Sandalphon found his sword hilt and brought out the long blade that he always kept by his side. It had the power of the Dunamis in it, the power of light to overcome the darkness. As soon as it was free of its scabbard, he swiped at the demon that held him, demon number three.

In his peripheral vision, he saw Mattatron slay the last creature and then fall to his knees, exhausted. Encouraged by his partner's victory, he sliced into the monster, creating a thick trench that soon overflowed with blood.

Though his attack was successful, it wasn't effective enough. The demon sank its sharp teeth deep into his neck, mauling him mercilessly. Sandalphon roared in agony, thrashing his head from side to side. His long white hair shook with the effort, and his face was transfigured with anguish.

Such excruciating pain fell upon him that his mind was paralysed for what seemed like an age. He fell backward, feeling the heavy weight of the dying demon on his chest. The two of them tumbled in a heap with him underneath.

Mattatron was at his side in a second, pulling the monster off him and grabbing his hand, but the world faded from view. He mouthed wordlessly at his companion, watching Mattatron stare in horror at him.

As he slipped away, he saw the Rescuer's luminescent face shining in the darkness, concerned but serene. His face sent warm rays of light into the back of Sandalphon's skull. Bathed in his presence, the Dunamis, Sandalphon, relaxed. "My dear servant Sandalphon. You fought well, but it's time for you to return home, to rest, and be renewed for a time. After your sojourn, we will travel together again. There is still work for you to do. Good work. I am with you both here and also there. I will not leave you. Take heart and rest now. Let my Dunamis bear you home."

The warrior angel went limp, leaving his companion holding his hand, alone with the bodies of four dead demons.

Mattatron caught his breath and stared at Sandalphon, tears in his eyes.

"We'll meet again, brother," he said. Sandalphon became a flash of chrysolite-green lightning that streaked up to the heavens and was gone.

Mattatron heard a quiet gasp to his right and realised the creature that had attacked his friend still had life in it. He pressed his ancient blade to its throat and shouted, "Tell me which dominion you are assigned to. I demand you tell me, in the name of the Rescuer."

Without opening its eyes, the creature snarled, "Griffton in England. Now let me die and depart."

"Who is your master? Who do you serve?" Silence.

"Tell me, I command you."

"Samyaza is my master. Samyaza will prevail." He rasped the words, his breathing becoming ragged.

"Samyaza of the two hundred Grigori? How many of you are assigned to Griffton? What is Samyaza's plan?"

But it was too late. The demon had died and gone back to the Earth. It had returned to Samyaza and to Griffton to ride on the back of a Dream Fighter of its choosing.

CAMERON GRINNED. He opened his hand and showed Rory half a dozen purple crystals.

"Hey, that's not fair. You've got two more than me," complained the younger brother. They were both dressed in blue jeans and red body-warmer jackets with matching backpacks and black trainers.

"We can find some more together. Then we'll both have six," said Cameron, his shaggy brown hair almost reaching his sparkling brown eyes.

"Okay. Let's go. Mum and Dad are talking, as always, and so's Micah."

"They're always talking."

They had fallen some way behind the grown-ups but were happily skipping across the red earth and purple stones. From time to time, they stopped when they spied a lizard or some other dream creature. Some animals in this land were multicoloured and shimmered in the strange light and walked busily from one point to another. Others had a dull hue and lay still by the rocks.

"Hey Rory, do you want to hear my rhyme? It's about the lizards we saw."

"Okay."

"It goes: *smiley, slimy, slippy lizards; super-silly, slinky lizards.*" Cameron grinned happily. "It's more of a tongue twister than a rhyme," he added.

"Can I have a go?"

"Of course!"

"Silly, stinky, sloppy lizards," Rory said slowly, trying to get the words right.

"That's not how it goes," complained Cameron.

"Do it again, then."

"It goes slimy, smiley, no hang on, smiley, slimy, slippy lizards; super-silly, slinky lizards. Like that."

"Oh, it's too hard," sulked Rory. Suddenly, he was scrambling on the ground. "I found one! I found one!" he cried.

He jumped up triumphantly with a huge amethyst-coloured crystal in his little hand. It caught the light of the red sun and made his palm and his wrist glow strangely.

"That's bigger than my ones! Can I have it?"

"No, I found it. You get your own."

"How about I swap it for two of mine?"

"No way."

"Three then."

"Hey Cam, look over there – it's water! A pool of water. We could have a paddle. Let's check it out?"

"What about mum and dad?"

"They could paddle too."

"No, I mean, what about if we get left behind?"

"They're not far, look. We'll catch up with them. They're too busy talking anyway."

"They're always busy talking," agreed Cameron.

Daniel and Arabella walked arm in arm, engaged in deep conversation with each other and with Micah, who stayed close to Daniel's side.

Daniel had chosen a path that led at right angles to the stone head, and for the past couple of days, they had walked and rested intermittently—though none of them seemed to feel tired. It was a strange phenomenon and something that created much conversation between the adults. They had met no one at all on their journey, which was remarkable, and the hills didn't seem to get any nearer despite the long hours of walking. Not until today, anyway. Today, the shade of the hills seemed within reach for the first time.

The strangest thing for the boys was that they didn't want to wee or eat. It amused them and made them quiz each other endlessly about whether it was time to go to the toilet yet.

Rory's joke was: "Knock knock. Who's there? Dunnap. Dunnap who? 'Done a poo?' Go to the toilet, then! But I don't want to!"

And so they had passed their first three days. Micah and Daniel had taken turns keeping watch while the others rested, not that their bodies needed to. It was more that their minds craved rest, and so they made provision and slept as they would normally, albeit a dreamless sleep.

"Race you to the water?" cried Rory. "You're on. Ready, set, go!"

The Harcourt boys sprinted off in the direction of the nearby pool. It shimmered under the purple sky, looking inky and inviting to the children. Only, as they approached it, the liquid seemed to boil away to be replaced by flat, red soil, just like the ground they had trodden between the stone head and here.

"Hey! Did you see that? It just went away," said Rory. "I think it's called a mirrarch."

"Like a mirror?"

"Something like that. It happens in the desert. But hold on, there's more water over there: an even bigger pool."

"Let's see if it's another mirrarch."

They travelled further. This, too, faded away, leaving the boys disappointed. But they soon spotted something else. It was a patch of ground with huge criss-cross markings on it, like a chessboard. There were coloured stones at some intersections and in the middle of certain squares. Some of the squares were a darker red than the others, but there didn't seem to be a discernible pattern.

"Do you think it's a game?" asked Rory.

"Yes. It's a game," nodded the taller boy.

"Let's play then."

"All right. You have that side, and I'll start on the other. What you do is hopscotch to the stones, and if you can pick them up from standing, you win them."

"Okay. What about if you fall over?"

"You go back to the start."

"All right. Let's go."

Cameron and Rory lined up at the edge of the grid. Around them, they imagined an audience of lizard creatures cheering them on. The crystals Rory was going for were blue and yellow, and Cameron's were rainbow coloured.

They stood in a place where the terrain was rocky and weedy. Brambly growths obscured their view of the distant hills to which the family was walking.

Cameron started first and hop-scotched to the nearest crystal. It was blue with a ruby tinge. He kept his balance and scooped up his prize. Rory, on the other hand, was overambitious and tumbled over, ripping his jeans at the knee. Although he didn't feel the pain, he felt uncomfortable, and his pride was hurt. In reality, he knew he had been greedy, trying to accumulate three gems in one go.

Pouting, he went back to the beginning as his brother watched him sternly to make sure he didn't cheat. Cameron then won another crystal, a fluorescent orange one. It was a major coup for him. Now back in the game, Rory hop-scotched an impressive distance and plucked a glowing gem of his own, holding it up proudly for Cameron to see.

"Well done!" said Cameron happily.

Their pockets were filling fast, and it was growing dark.

"I think we should get back to mum and dad. We can have a race. Can you see them?"

They looked around, peering into the distance. "Nope. Can you?" asked Rory.

"Not me. But I think they went that way, towards the hills."

"Let's go then!"

"Hang on, I think my foot's stuck."

"What do you mean, Cam?"

Cameron looked down in alarm at his left foot. It was wedged into the ground, up to his ankle. "I can't get it out, Rory. I think I'm stuck in the mud."

"But it isn't mud!"

Rory ran over to the place where his brother was standing and tugged at his trouser leg.

"Hey! Don't pull!"

"Does it hurt?"

"Not really: I can't feel anything much, but I can't get it out."

"What do you mean?"

"Like it's stuck in the sand, just like when we covered dad at the beach, remember?"

"What shall I do?" asked Rory, tears in his eyes.

"You run and get mum as quick as you can. She'll know what to do." Cameron stopped trying to twist his foot out of the ground and sat down, bending his knees.

"Which way?"

"That way, silly. And hurry."

"I'll get mum. You'll be okay." Rory ran off between the brambly bushes, towards the faraway hills, looking concerned.

Back at the strange chessboard, Cameron cried freely now, away from the gaze of his younger brother.

CHAPTER 14

Micah was the first to realise the children hadn't kept pace. He halted the party as they approached a group of plum-coloured hills in the shape of a horseshoe.

Daniel and Arabella were dismayed that they had ignored their children for so long. Ashen-faced, Daniel bit back his old nature, which was to blame Arabella. The truth was, he was equally to blame, and he would only attack her out of guilt.

Instead, he felt the Dunamis reassuring him and calmly said, "Let's go back and look for them. I expect they've found something interesting to play with."

They trotted back in the direction they had come from, and it wasn't long before they met the little manly figure of Rory racing towards them. His hair flopped as he ran.

"Daniel laughed, relieved. "Rory! I knew you were all right. But where's Cameron?"

The young boy flew into Arabella's arms and wrapped his legs around her waist, burying his face in her shoulder. He started to cry.

"Tell me what happened," she said.

Rory blurted out, "Cam's stuck in the mud. Only it isn't

mud. We were playing, and we got left behind. He's stuck and can't get free. It's his foot."

"Slow down," said Daniel. "Are you all right?" Rory nodded.

"Whereabouts were you playing?" Rory indicated with his head.

"Take us there," said Daniel.

Together, they ran back to the red chessboard, crossing the dry red land with its cracks and boulders. Daniel and Arabella rushed over to their son and put their arms around him, kissing him. For a moment, Cameron was completely covered in their embraces.

"We are so sorry," Arabella cried. "We didn't realise you weren't with us. Forgive us? Please."

"Oh, Mum," said Cameron. He looked weary.

Daniel started to score the ground around Cameron's ankle with a sharp rock.

"Hold still, son, this shouldn't take too long." Chipping into the hard soil was slow work, and it was growing dark. The alien sun had reached the mountains, leaving behind a beetroot-stained world. Rory sat down next to Cameron and put his arm around him, staring at the ground.

"Is it working?" Arabella asked Daniel.

"I think it's going to take a bit of time to dig him out, and the sun's going in. We might have to spend the night here, but I will get him out."

"How long do you think it will take, Daniel?"

"I don't know, Arabella," snapped Daniel. Then he said, more gently, "Let's seek the Dunamis together?"

The others nodded, and they closed their eyes in unison. In seconds, they felt surrounded by the warmth and peace of the Dunamis. Their striving and anxious thoughts ceased, and they all relaxed, including Cameron. Rory started giggling. They were left with a thick sense of hope.

Micah opened his eyes and smiled. His angelic face was radiant, and he emanated a supreme confidence that reassured the group.

"I think I know what we need to do," he said.

He stood at the edge of the chessboard, looking at the strange crystals that lay at the intersections or near the centre of particular squares. "Let me see now. Yes, this might work."

Arabella looked up at him quizzically. She was still kneeling on the ground next to Cameron, with her arm around her son.

"Did you boys shift any of these crystals here? Did you take any of them? I'm not telling anyone off here, so just tell me if you did."

"We were playing a game, like hopscotch, where we hopped over to the crystals and picked them up if we could," Cameron told him.

"It's not stealing, is it, Micah?" asked Rory.

"No, it's not stealing," laughed Micah.

"I've got some in my pocket," Cameron confessed. He extracted them and then showed them to Micah in the fading light.

"Me too," Rory chimed in.

"Okay, the next thing is, do you remember exactly where you got them from? I think we need to put them back where they were. Quickly."

"Why?" Rory enquired.

"It's a bit like putting a game away back in its box."

"Oh, okay," said Rory.

"Do you think you can remember where you got your crystals from?"

"I think so, for some of them. I know I got this orange one from there, and you can still see the hole in the ground where it came from."

"Good. Do your best to put them all back and I think we're going to be fine. Trust the Dunamis to lead you if you're not sure."

"Okay."

"Good. Let's go," he said kindly but with some urgency in his voice. Darkness was approaching fast from the direction of the distant stone head. It was like a lumbering monster coming to devour them.

"THIS WAY," said the Dunamis. Rachel almost missed his voice because she was distracted by a dark-blue flying creature circling the sky above her. It looked like a huge buzzard or even a prehistoric Pterodactyl, she thought, with a massive wingspan and bony limbs. It emitted a high-pitched shriek that echoed around the skies.

"Rescuer?" she said, looking around, confused.

"This way," repeated the Dunamis. His voice was like the wind blowing across the hills. It was the first time she had heard his voice for herself, though she remembered Caleb could hear him and Daniel, too.

She was at the far edge of the broad valley where she had met the Rescuer, discovered the waterfall, and bumped into her father. The tall cliff wall had given way to another valley, a depression many hundreds of miles across. This basin was edged with distant mountains that looked hazy, being so far away. Down in the valley were bushy green and purple trees that looked like thousands of broccoli heads. However, in reality, they were ten times the size of trees on Earth.

There was a clear, broad path into the valley, a red soil ribbon that wound down and disappeared into the undergrowth. It wasn't this path the Dunamis was showing to her. She felt he was urging her to turn left and pass between two trees. But she couldn't see anything beyond them.

"Are you sure? Shouldn't I be going down through this valley? How am I going to find my friends?"

She was faced with complete silence but knew she had received her orders and had a decision to make.

"All right then, we'll go this way if you want."

Rachel skipped over a root and found herself descending a steep hill and entering a forest of thick trees with trunks covered with gnarly black bark.

A series of paths led through the woods. As she walked along the forest floor, the ebony columns hemmed her in, forcing her to move forward like a rat in a maze. Left, then right, then right, then left.

Every so often, she came to a fork and had to choose one path over another, which was vexing. She forgot to seek the Dunamis at these times and soon got completely lost, encountering one dead-end after another and having to retrace her steps.

The trees all looked the same, tall with long branches ending in purple bushes, which intertwined above her head. The red sun shone through the gaps, affording just enough light to see the way.

At first, she walked quickly, enjoying the sweet presence of the Dunamis. He was her new friend, someone who loved her completely and accompanied her wherever she went. He poured joy into her heart and filled her with a boldness to explore. She brushed her hands across the trees every so often, enjoying the roughness of the bark.

The maroon soil was littered with strange dark shells, a version of the horse chestnut, thought Rachel. But when she stooped to pick them up, the casings were soft rather than prickly and seemed moist, and this put her off picking up any more of them. They felt like they were alive, and it reminded her of the creatures that Olm seemed so fond of.

She lost track of her surroundings, having taken a left, a right, and two lefts in succession, or had that been two rights? She wasn't sure. A fear fell on her suddenly, along with a panic that she would be lost for good in the maze. She rushed along now, feeling the need to get out of the enclosure and see the daylight again.

At yet another dead-end, Rachel spied a lizard in a tree, a large, pale creature covered in desiccated scales. It jumped between two branches, and she froze and stared at it. She was convinced it was about to leap at her face. Its lizard eyes regarded her coolly, and she thought again of Olm, the horrible albino boy who lived with Zed in the creepy wooden house.

"Must keep moving," she said out loud. The creature stayed still, and she passed by, finding herself in a long corridor with hefty black tree trunks.

"Oh, Dunamis," she heard herself saying out loud again. "I'm lost. Will you help me?"

A wave of peace surged through her, and he said, "Do not be anxious. The old Rachel is dead; the new one is alive, so do not fear. Take the next left, then left again."

"I hear you, Dunamis," said Rachel solemnly and then again with a laugh, "I really can hear you, Dunamis!"

"So, follow me," he said gently.

Sure enough, Rachel made two left turns, and the trees parted to open up a beautiful vista displaying a lush valley teeming with plant life. The overarching purple sky tinted the brown and red treetops with its unique hue, and the hazy mountains could be seen again a great distance away. The same ribbon of water she had seen before shimmered at the centre of the valley, snaking far off to a set of distant caves.

It was a brand-new world, unseen by human eyes and waiting to be discovered and explored. Rachel felt the gravity and honor of the moment, wishing Lara were there to share it with her—or Iona or even Lake.

Rachel sighed, her heart leaping. Her body was still buzzing with the aftermath of the liquid fire that had coursed through her veins: the fire that had seared her but left her stronger.

"This way?" she asked.

"This way," he echoed. As she started to walk down into the sumptuous scene, more words formed in her mind. Each time she heard his voice, it became more and more familiar to her, a sweet, voiceless voice that touched her heart.

The words were: "Rachel, call on me and trust me when things look impossible, and remember, don't be afraid. Remember, I am with you now. You can always talk to me, always call on me."

Rachel grinned.

MICAH'S PLAN worked out well, and Rory placed the last crystal at the intersection. Rory had made plenty of mistakes, arguing with Cameron from time to time about the best place to put the crystals back. He was reluctant to give up the big amethyst as well but knew he had to. In the end, they remembered how the game had played out, and all the colourful rocks were returned to their original places.

With no fanfare or warning, Cameron suddenly realised he could lift his trapped foot out of the ground. Micah and Rory had done it. They had unlocked the puzzle of the mean chessboard.

Crying again, Cameron stood up and embraced his parents properly.

"I don't like this place anymore," he said. "I want to go home."

His parents didn't say anything. Daniel stared into the distance as the mountains were swallowed up by the shadows.

Then he said, "Let's spend the night here. Micah, you take the first watch. Arabella, you go second. I'll do the third, and in the morning, we'll head for the hills and carry on looking for Rachel. If she's trapped, like my little man was, she's going to be desperate by now. We need to find her."

CHAPTER 15

Rachel had detected movement a while ago while walking through the valley. She was right. The sandy head of a big cat appeared from behind a tree. It looked small because it was so far away, but she was pretty sure it was a leopard. She remembered it from school.

"Is that a leopard: that thing with the fuzzy spots all over it?" Rachel asked the Dunamis.

"Is it safe?" she added. "It looks cute. Cute but dangerous. I'm not really a cat person, though." A memory flashed through her mind. It was of the panther that attacked her in the hospital last year. She recalled its red eyes and shuddered.

The leopard's body brushed through the foliage as it moved from one hiding place to another. It stayed still, becoming almost invisible against the undergrowth.

Rachel watched it coming closer from a great distance away, snaking ever so slowly through the long, tufty fronds. It was a sleek and curvaceous creature with distinctive black semi-circles dotting its sand-coloured fur and face. At one point, she gasped as she saw its whole body, a sandy mirage against a sea of green leaves.

Rachel's wonder turned to fear. She realised she was its prey: the one being hunted.

"Is that thing after me? What do I do?"

She started to back away, finding a path that led away to the left as it twisted down into the valley. Keeping the leopard in view, Rachel carried on walking backwards, trying not to trip over. It was slow going because the ground was uneven, with thick wedges of growth all over the place.

"I really don't like big cats. Little ones are okay, but not big ones. I hate panthers in particular. Lions are fine because it's like they don't really exist except for the zoo." She was aware she was babbling uncontrollably to keep herself from panicking.

She saw the creature's head bob upwards, and its ears twitch as she backed away. It sniffed the air. Rachel carried on treading lightly, then found the confidence to turn around and walk a little faster.

She covered a lot of ground in a short space of time, making it to a large clump of trees that gave her shelter. She stopped and peered around a huge coal-black tree trunk. The leopard was no longer in sight. Rachel held her breath and scanned the horizon. Her eyes landed on every sand-coloured feature: a patch of tall, dry grass, a stretch of dry ground, or a gap in the bark of a tree where the black covering had fallen away to reveal lighter flesh. The leopard was nowhere to be seen.

She waited a moment longer and then went on her way, walking around a set of five thick trees whose lowest boughs began high above her head. If she saw the leopard again and needed to escape, climbing the trees wasn't an option.

As she walked away from her covering, the valley opened up before her again with the beautiful shimmering river in the far distance, twisting down towards a set of caves.

She carried on, stepping carefully and quietly so as not to attract feline attention.

She walked past another set of trees with a broad stretch of saplings, thin, grey growths that protruded straight upwards into the air, reaching for the sky.

Mustard-coloured grassland lay beyond the saplings, and this continued for many acres. The rolling hills were covered in thick, straw-like grass that undulated every so often with a breeze she couldn't feel. In the distance, the water glimmered invitingly.

Rachel was striding with confidence now, seeing nothing of danger for miles around. She was safe here in the middle of this expansive grassland, just her, the tall grass, and the red sky. Glancing absently over to her right, she thought she saw the head of the big cat. It looked like a light orange football surrounded by tall grass of a paler hue. If it was the leopard, then it had found the perfect camouflage.

She walked gingerly on, keeping her eyes set on the place where she thought she had seen her foe several hundred feet to her right.

She had nowhere to hide now and was fully exposed in this field. The trees were far away, and the mountains were a hazy blur beyond the caves, which grinned at her like a line of mouldy teeth.

It was definitely the head of a leopard, dappled with black prints and those unmistakable eyes. It was tracking her stealthily, effortlessly keeping pace as she travelled. It was now a hundred feet closer than it was before.

She kept going, feeling it was better to stay on the move. However, the next set of trees and bushes was still too far away to reach in a hurry.

The breeze picked up, and this time, she felt it caress her cheeks as she saw the tall grass move under its guidance. "It's just like the wind on Earth, back home," she thought.

"I'm going to die," said Rachel out loud, her old nature rising. She felt like a defenceless fawn, unable to escape. The panther from last year filled her mind. It had jumped at her twice: once through a glass window and the second time down a hospital stairwell. She imagined it happening a third time: a big cat closing in for the kill.

"I'm going to die," she concluded with a firm nod.

RACHEL QUICKENED HER PACE, trudging through the long grass. She lengthened her strides but noticed that the cat was effortlessly keeping pace with her. Starting to panic, she broke into a trot, knowing full well that the leopard was still likely to be a lot faster than her.

Suddenly, the creature decided to show her the extent of its power. It bounded across from several hundred feet away, springing like a gazelle, focused completely on her. She saw its strong, bulky body ripple as it moved. It was a creature of beauty and might. Its whole body was covered in distinctive black marks, which looked like tiny paw prints on a sandy beach.

It was almost within leaping distance of her, and Rachel's mind flipped back to the dark memory of the panther attack from last year. She remembered freezing as the panther leapt at her, fearing she would be mauled to death.

Once again, her mind went completely blank as the big cat closed in for the kill with a growl. All she could think about was the pain that was about to engulf her, coupled with her impending death. She remembered reading somewhere that leopards like to drag their prey up trees and finish them there. She felt her corpse was about to be pulled a long way back to the tree line.

Then she remembered the Dunamis. "What do I do?" She panted.

One word came in reply: "Laugh."

"Laugh? Did you just say laugh?" She thought she'd misheard the command from her new friend.

"My joy is your strength," he replied.

The leopard bounded over to her and bared its fangs. At the

top and bottom corners of its wide, open mouth, it had long, pointed teeth, with a row of half a dozen smaller ones between each set of fangs. Two greenish eyes stared at her, surrounded by long white whiskers that fanned out in all directions.

Rachel saw nothing to laugh about, and it seemed contrary to how she was feeling right now. But she whispered, "Okay, Dunamis, I'm going to try this."

Rachel made herself laugh. "Ah-ha! Huh-huh! Ha-ha!" she began. As she embarked on the wild exercise, an overwhelming joy rose in her heart and swamped her. She felt like she had gone under the surface of a lake, and her whole body had been drenched.

She laughed again, but this time, it was from her heart, a deep belly laugh that couldn't help but find its expression vocally.

"Ha ha! Ha-ha-ha!" The sound of her own laughter surprised her.

She found it hard to stop, and the leopard rocked back on its haunches for a few moments and then sat down in the long grass. Its tail rose and started to sway slowly. Before long, it lost interest in Rachel and began licking its lips and looking around. The Dunamis spoke. "Your weapons are laughter and faith. Remember this."

"Okay, Dunamis," Rachel laughed, tears in her eyes.

She smiled and wondered as the cat got up and padded away, back the way it had come. Soon, it was a dot in the distance, and then it was gone completely.

Rachel stood in the vast grassy expanse, staring into the distance, clutching her stomach and giggling. She brimmed with a new confidence, enjoying the Dunamis more than anything else she could remember.

Finally, she decided it was time to carry on her journey and search for the Harcourt family.

"This way?" she asked.

"This way," echoed the Dunamis.

THE HARCOURT FAMILY finally arrived at the hills that had eluded them for so long. Large creatures soared far above them, flying between the stretch of ground between the hills and the mountains.

"They look like dinosaurs," said Rory.

"Pterodactyls. Definitely pterodactyls," said Cameron studiously.

"How do you know? Have you ever seen one?"

"I have now," he told his brother. "That's how I know."

They both listened as the animals called to each other with terrifying screeches.

They had spent an uneventful night at the chessboard and walked as quickly as the boys allowed them, resting the minimum so they could reach the hills.

Meanwhile, they kept a keen lookout for Rachel through the valley to their right while also looking to the left between the peaks. Nobody wanted to voice the fear that they wouldn't be able to find her in this massive kingdom. Instead, they kept to the plan, looking, talking, and watching for any sign of human life, with five pairs of eyes tuned in to the movement.

"If I were Rachel, I'd try to walk to the hills," Micah said. "That valley looks far too dangerous with all those rocks hanging in the air. The air is much clearer here."

"Well, I hope you're right," said Daniel.

"I wonder how the house is," Arabella said out of the blue.

"I know, darling. But it's no use worrying about it."

"I'm not worrying. I'm just saying I wonder how it is. Okay, I am worrying about it. Those mindless thugs. I expect there's broken glass all over my rugs, and they've probably taken my jewellery."

"I'll buy you more."

Arabella snapped, "I don't care about the jewellery."

"I know." Daniel put his arm around his wife as they walked. "I know," he said again.

Meanwhile, Micah was playing a word game with Cameron. It was a crazy rhyming game that Cameron had made up called *Tokanooze*. It seemed to lack any formal rules, as far as Arabella could make out. However, Micah insisted it had an inner logic.

"Tokanooze," said Micah. "Dogadooze," replied Cameron. Micah snapped, "Hogalooze."

"You just lose," said Cameron, grinning. "Okay, you win."

"Let me play?" insisted Rory.

"You don't know the rules," said Cameron.

"Yes, I do."

"I'll play with you," Micah suggested, and so it went on. He dropped back behind Daniel and Arabella.

After a while, the distance between the two groups grew longer, and the children's merry game receded.

Arabella turned to Daniel and said, "He's so good with the kids."

"Yes, he is, isn't he?"

"Do you remember when he first came to us? He was so formal. I expect he was scared of you."

"Of course he was. So he should be," laughed Daniel. Then he became serious. "I'm not proud of the things I did and the things I involved him in. If I could do it all over again, well, you know. But it shows the strength of his character that he's forgiven me and chosen to stay attached to our family."

"We are his family," replied Arabella. "When grandfather adopted him, he made it very clear he was to be one of us, although he made up that role of assistant when he became a teenager."

"That's right."

"Then, when he worked with Father, he kept on doing good work and seemed happy with it. He's been with you since he was, what, fifteen?"

"Sixteen. It's only been two years, Bella. I expect the first year with me was a dark one for him, though he doesn't talk about it much."

"I don't blame him. You were so secretive then."

"I never got him to do anything illegal. Well, not directly. But still, I regret involving him."

"But then we met the Dunamis after you did, both him and me, in your study that time. It's been a year since then. You're completely different, and so is he. He's become lighter, just like you. He's not so serious all the time."

Daniel smiled. "He was a very serious young man, wasn't he?"

"Intense. Like you." She leaned over and kissed him on the cheek.

"Yeah, just like me." Daniel pulled a serious face, then laughed.

DANIEL AND ARABELLA found a series of red-stone caves beyond the hills, but it was difficult for them to keep the boys under control. They kept tearing off and ducking into one cave after the next in search of treasure and adventure. Squealing with delight, the children left the adults for many long, anxious moments.

"Boys," Daniel barked as they ran into yet another cave. "Keep us in sight at all times. We don't know where these go or what's inside them. Be safe, for goodness' sake."

"I'll go and get them this time," volunteered Micah. He strode into the cave to bring the boys out. The cave mouth was a wide semicircle. It was made of thick slabs of smooth red and grey stone that merged with the hard ground beneath. The cave was inviting, especially for the younger contingent, and the red sunshine lit up the inner walls. The boys ran further in, exploring an interconnected area, and could no longer be heard.

Micah was gone for a long time, and Daniel and Arabella

waited nervously for the three of them. At long last, the boys trotted out, oblivious to the fact that they were waiting for them, and wanted hugs from their parents.

"We found a silver wall and a pool of water, but it was dark," jabbered Rory, the younger one.

"Where's Micah?" asked Cameron. "Isn't he out here?"

"He went in to look for you troublesome two," said Daniel. "I'm sure he'll be out in a minute. What else did you find in there?"

"There's nothing much, really. Further inside, it's dark and smells a bit strange. There aren't any monsters, I don't think."

There was a sudden yell from the cave: Micah's voice. It sounded like he was in pain. Daniel called for him and then rushed towards the entrance.

"Micah? Micah!"

Micah wandered out slowly, looking dazed. They saw that Micah's head was bleeding.

"Are you all right?" Daniel quickly enquired.

Micah didn't say anything but put a hand to his head and stared through his almond-shaped eyes. He had blood in his wavy hair, and his shoulders were hunched.

"Did you bash your head?" asked Rory. Micah nodded.

"Here, take this and press it to the cut," said Arabella, giving him a tissue from a packet. Micah took it absent-mindedly and pressed it to his head.

"No, not there, dear. Move it a bit lower, that's right."

They fussed around Micah, making him sit down on a rock. The children fiddled with his hair, twirling it and making it stick up. Meanwhile, Arabella checked his cut, which had stopped bleeding. Eventually, he was okay to go on.

"Good man," said Daniel. "Good man," he repeated.

This time, when they set off, they made sure to have the children, as well as poor Micah, close by them.

CHAPTER 16

Rachel wandered through the fields of wafting grass and down the hills that paved the valley. Gorgeous grassland yielded to red-soiled scrubland, which gave way to a mossy path that wound ever onwards. The caves grew nearer, though the mountains kept their distance, and Rachel found streams of water snaking through the land.

She discovered a cool stream to paddle in, holding her trainers in her hand with her socks tucked inside. She enjoyed the feeling of the water on her bare skin and the pleasant texture of smooth stones under her toes.

The breeze blew her hair about her face, and she enjoyed seeing the white strands floating into sight every so often. Her platinum hair was better than the black hair she used to have, she mused. No doubt Iona would love it and even say she should dye it blue or red or several colours at the same time. She liked it white, though. It was a visible reminder of her meeting with the Rescuer: a badge of honour.

She climbed onto the bank because the streams were growing deeper as they joined the river that ran down towards the caves.

The caves were made of dark red rock with indentations that

scored the surface of their smooth outer walls. Some of them had intricate patterns formed by beetroot-coloured vines with tendrils that crisscrossed each other, intimately entwined.

Rachel peered into the ragged entrances, trying to have a good look inside, though they were still many metres away. But she could see nothing of note inside, just darkness.

"Where am I going?" she asked. There was no answer from the Dunamis.

She carried on walking beside the streams, parallel to the caves, which were still some distance away. However, she was close enough to them she couldn't see anything beyond anymore, although she knew the mountains sat several miles behind and stretched to the left and right.

Feeling weary, Rachel sat down by the stream on a mossy rock and looked around her. A couple of bright red creatures were flying around. She'd seen them earlier, but they had vanished for the past hour.

Although they moved like butterflies, they were more like bubbles, round, eccentric creatures that had their own spherical force fields that caught the light of the ruby sun. This gave them their sheen.

She looked more closely and saw that they had delicate reptilian bodies and lidless eyes. They had no apparent means of steering themselves, like wings or limbs. They were just helpless, aimless bubbles that floated on the wind.

"You are strange little things, aren't you?" she commented. Then she asked again, "Where am I going?"

Unfortunately, the response she got was that she should head for the caves next.

"But I don't want to go into those caves. They look a bit dark." She looked suspiciously at them, seeing how the red sunlight hit the entrance and highlighted the soil at the base of the cave but little else beyond that. Then she sat sulking on her mossy rock and staring at the stream.

Looking up, she saw something appear at the top of the line

of caves. It was a dark cloud appearing on the horizon, which formed into a figure of a bear or, perhaps, a large man. Seconds later, the creature sprouted large black wings and stood to its full height, chest thrust forward. It was a bulky, imposing figure, reminiscent of a superhero—or perhaps a supervillain—a massive man-like being draped in a sleek black costume. The transformation was startling, its presence dominating the space around it.

Horror-struck, Rachel gasped, unable to drag her eyes away.

With no warning, the monster sprang from its perch at the top of the precipice and launched itself in her direction. As it put its arms out, its leathery wings stretched to display an impressive wingspan.

The creature floated gracefully down to the bottom of the cave and landed on two enormous feet. It had talons like a great eagle and the ferocious teeth of a beast. Dark eyes stared across the distance at Rachel.

There was nowhere to hide.

The monster walked slowly and confidently towards Rachel without taking its eyes off her, like something out of the darkest horror movie. She started to whimper and back away from the stream.

"This is not happening," she said. "I am in a dream, in a dream world that doesn't exist. This thing isn't real. My mind is playing tricks on me."

She glanced around her, desperately trying to find somewhere to hide, a tree to climb, or a hole to disappear into. Out here in the open, she was completely exposed. Panic gripped her heart. The creature continued to move towards her resolutely. It seemed in no hurry, knowing she was no match. She was easy prey for a quick kill.

SOMETIMES, he slept without dreaming, and at other times, he was forced to endure one cinematic dream after another. A dozen scenarios in a row often unfolded relentlessly, with him as both the star and the victim.

In this one, Caleb Noble was back in Slovakia. The Dream Fighters captured him and locked him in a small cell with a view of the forest through wooden bars. But this time, the Dunamis was not with him, and he was alone and friendless.

They beat him with fists and chains, and one of his captors put a cigarette out on his cheek. The pain of it was shocking, and he cried aloud. They sneered at him and pulled his hair. He called out for the Dunamis, but he was utterly alone and abandoned. He died slowly from his internal injuries and spiralled to his grave.

In the next dream, he was again captured by Dream Fighters at the top of a mountain. Ice and snow whipped at him mercilessly, tearing into his flesh. They tortured him, bound him to a rock, and took his shirt from him, leaving him exposed to the elements. The tiny barbs of ice bit into him as the storm gathered pace. He could feel the freezing fingers ravage his naked torso. Eventually, the harsh weather picked his flesh apart. Eviscerated, his warmth drained away, and he endured a slow and painful death.

During these dreams, aware that they were dreams, his will to live ebbed away, and his mind screamed for an end. But this was denied him, and so he remained in this half-living, half-dying state, mocked by the world, abandoned by his Creator, with no end in sight. His faith in anything good was being stripped away methodically, minute by minute, hour by hour.

IT WAS ONLY when the demon creature was within feet of her that Rachel remembered the lesson with the leopard. At first, her mind was blank as it crossed the streams and stones, but it finally shocked itself back into action. She realised she needed to laugh out loud.

Blinded by panic, she stared at the monster. It was huge and tall. Its broad, thick wings were made of leather, and its bulky body was covered in layers of fat. Two powerful arms were ready to grab her, and, like its feet, these also ended in sharp talons, eager to tear into her skin. She felt pain across her body in anticipation of being stabbed, and her brain was clouded with fear.

Worst of all was its face. Its intense, dark eyes locked onto hers, unblinking and full of malice. A fang-filled mouth gaped hungrily, the jagged teeth ready to tear into her. Inside, a slick, black tongue moved repulsively, slithering within the cavernous maw as though tasting the air in anticipation of her flesh.

Suddenly, Rachel laughed a nervous laugh, squeezing it out from somewhere inside her. She then forced a louder sound out, which was both alien and surprising.

The beast rushed at her, knocking her to the ground with one hand. She felt the pain of the blow on her cheek and hit the back of her head on a rock. Blinding pain flashed through her skull.

It hadn't worked. The laughter hadn't worked.

She lay there in shock as the creature stood back to admire its handiwork. She closed her eyes and yielded what she considered to be her final thought, saying out loud, "Dunamis, it didn't work. I can't do it. Help!"

Time stood still, and the words that filled her mind were "laughter and faith." Her body was filled in an instant with warmth, the presence of the Rescuer's Dunamis, and she remembered his words. "Follow the Dunamis and have faith in him. He will lead and protect you."

The love and hope of the Dunamis poured into her.

Rachel opened her eyes, seeing the demon creature bow down to finish her. It brought its horrible face close to hers and snarled.

This time, trusting the Dunamis to protect her, she found it within herself to laugh, bizarre and incongruous joy bubbling up within her.

"Ha ha! Ha ha hah!"

The creature straightened up and gazed at her.

"I'm either going to die or not. Either way, it's funny. Ha ha hah!" Rachel said, feeling completely mad.

The nightmare creature crumpled to its knees, its heavy weight collapsing onto the rocks. Its hideous head cracked into the ground and lay still.

"Ha ha! It worked! But how?" laughed Rachel.

Then she saw why the creature had fallen. Towering above them both was another winged creature, but this one was dressed in white robes. Rachel saw his sword wedged into the back of the demon, and its handle was sticking out at right angles.

She stared at the white figure with her huge brown eyes and caught her breath, awe-struck.

She had never seen anything like him in real life—if you could even call this real life. This being, so strikingly beautiful and human-like, yet clearly not human, stood before her. The angel—and he was clearly an angel—radiated serenity and composure. He exuded an aura of immense power and glory, his presence almost overwhelming. It was as if he glowed with an inner light, illuminating the space around him with a gentle, ethereal brilliance.

"Thank you mister…" she said.

"Mattatron. My name is Mattatron. I have been tracking this one, but your faith has brought me closer. That's how it works. In the moment, the Dunamis pairs us together, you and me. A moment is all we need. A moment can be a tipping point, the switch from defeat to victory. Your choice is which way you turn: towards or away from the one who can help. Remember that, Rachel Race."

The angel had penetrating eyes, an innocent expression, and

long white hair, like the Rescuer. She felt she'd seen him before, but this was clearly nonsense.

Then, searching her memory, she remembered him as being one of the figures from her dream in Griffton General, a man who travelled with the Rescuer. This was one of the King's companions, a warrior from a distant age.

She wanted to ask him about the creature and this strange land and reached for the words, but they didn't come.

Instead, Mattatron seemed to anticipate her questions and said, "What is this creature? I think you know the answer to that."

She carried on staring at the angel, transfixed.

"Now, young lady, I must leave you. I have work to do. As for you, follow the Dunamis, and perhaps our paths will cross again."

Mattatron, powerful and muscular, spread his white wings and soared into the air, quickly disappearing over the tops of the caves. Rachel was used to seeing the seagulls take off and land in Griffton. Although this was vaguely like that, it was, in reality, like nothing she had seen. The combination of his strength and grace made it an incredible sight. She looked for a long time at the top of the rocks where the angel had gone, but he didn't reappear.

Rachel looked down at the dead creature. It had taken on a grey hue and, thankfully, lay unmoving. She shivered and walked past its body.

"Right, so you want me to go into the caves, do you, Dunamis?" She sensed an affirmative. "As long as you can still make me laugh when I'm in danger, I'll do it."

So, she trod gingerly over the stream, stepping over the pebbles and stones, and, finding a path down through what was left of the valley, walked towards the caves.

She allowed herself one last look across the open land, taking in the wide bank up to the open fields with the long, thick grass and trees that dotted the horizon like miniature spikes. Her eyes followed the winding streams that connected the river to the upper lands. She imagined for a moment that she was standing on Mars, the red planet, the world's first female astronaut sent to another world. Beyond the valley lay the deep basin, Rachel's Pool, and the waterfall and the lake her dad had fallen into.

He was out there somewhere, in this strange mezzanine land, transformed and strengthened by the Rescuer and making his own way, no doubt. Although she was curious and, in fact, eager to see him again, she knew things would unfold at their own pace and in their own strange order.

Gathering her courage, she turned and climbed up into the mouth of the cave, scrambling up the red rocks to the entrance. The gap in the rock wall was about ten feet high, and she easily passed through it.

Rachel took a deep breath and ventured into the darkness.

MICAH HAD BEEN silent on the journey past the caves, and Arabella was fretting. He walked behind her and Daniel, keeping the children company as they chatted to each other, but he seemed subdued and unwilling to play their word games.

"Do you think he's okay, Dan? I'm worried about him after that bump he had."

"You know what he's like, Bella. Sometimes, he's quiet. He likes to spend time thinking, like me."

"I suppose so." Arabella looked serious. After a while, she added, "Okay, Daniel. As long as you think he's all right. You know him better than me."

They had come to another part of the land where the rocks were hanging in the air again, just as they had when they first came out of the stone head. The huge boulders levitated and twisted in space, starting at head height and then going up many metres into the air.

Daniel tried putting his hand up to pull one down. It was

solid and jagged, but he seemed happy where it was, and he was unable to extract it from its place. He could, however, turn it around slowly and look at its many faces and crevices.

Cameron commented, "Wow, Dad! It's just like an asteroid belt."

"Can we climb them, Dad?" pleaded Rory.

"Yeah, let's see how high we can go!" said Cameron. "Can you help us up, Dad?"

"No, children, it's too dangerous. If you fall, you'll hurt yourselves. We don't want that," Arabella said gently.

The boys relented, and they all walked on.

Eventually, the travellers came to the end of their path, and a wall made of solid rock prevented them from going any further. Their options were to travel back towards the valley that they were skirting, with its formidable terrain and twisting paths, or explore the caves.

The only problem was that the valley looked dangerous, with long fissures and cracks that seemed to open up to nothingness beneath. In some places, the ways appeared to be impassable because of these gaping chasms.

Although it might be possible to pick a path through the minefield of cracks, Daniel could see that some of the gaps in the path were too big for the children to cross. Short of giving them piggybacks, he wasn't confident of the journey through the valley. Daniel and Arabella stood and looked at each other for a while, trying to decide what to do.

Then, they heard a sound from inside the nearest cave. It sounded like a human voice, a low moan echoing around the cave complex and finally dribbling out to them. Somebody was in pain; horrible, wounded pain.

There was a long moment, and then a voice said, "Stop, please stop. Leave me alone. No more. I can't take any more. Let me die."

"I think I know that voice," said Daniel. "I definitely know that voice. You're going to think I'm crazy, but this whole place is crazy."

"Go on," urged Arabella.

"That sounds like Caleb. Caleb Noble, if I'm not mistaken."

"Are you sure?"

There was another anguished cry.

"Micah, what do you think?" called Daniel.

Micah stared, his eyes bloodshot and his wavy hair caked with dry blood. He nodded and waved his hand in the air, signalling that they should go in and investigate.

"Hold on a minute," said Daniel. He swung his bulky rucksack off his back, opened it, and pulled out a small flashlight. Switching it on, he shone it on the children's faces and grinned. "What do you reckon, boys?"

"Arabella, I've got one for you too. Here. And boys, remember there are lights on your key rings?"

Then he commanded, "Okay, let's go in. Micah, you come with me. Arabella, follow us with the kids, but keep back a little, just in case."

CHAPTER 17

The caves were dark and vast, each footstep and breath echoing endlessly through the labyrinth of chambers. The reverberating sounds hinted at the sheer size of the complex, a sprawling maze of rooms that seemed to stretch on forever into the blackness. The boys tried whispering, talking, and calling, only to be hushed by the adults. But their voices had already escaped and rushed around the caverns like ghosts who were free at last.

Daniel shone his light on the ground before them, then at the walls, trying to get a sense of space and to determine whether it was safe to move forward. At the same time, Arabella and the boys shot their beams in different directions, with the boys frequently trying to blind each other and laughing. They played cops, making a midnight bust in Death City, and laughed a little too much.

Again, the adults tried desperately to keep them quiet. The ground seemed damp but firm enough. A mixture of hard mud and rock stretched from wall to wall. The first cave was high and capacious, with a huge distance between the outer entrance and the next opening. The walls were unmarked except for a series of light diagonal lines that ran from top to bottom.

The children felt the cold and buttoned up, but they didn't complain. The party moved from one roomy space to another.

They could still hear voices, one or two more joining the first. Daniel estimated that there were three people moaning and talking. One had a low, manly voice, and Daniel imagined this to be Caleb. The others were higher and frailer. Mostly, they heard moaning and followed this as best they could through the complex of caves. Whether natural or man-made, the rooms were easy to traverse, though they came across many dead-ends and frequently had to retrace their steps.

Finally, the voices grew louder. Daniel led his family out of a long, low-ceilinged area and into a much larger one with a broad, shiny pool of liquid at the side. At the far end of this room, they saw three hunched figures sitting at the base of the wall, hugging their legs with their arms. The first was muscular, the second was well-built but slimmer and older, and the third was thin and tall.

On top of the head of each one was a bloated creature made of dark, translucent jelly with tendrils that stretched down around the jaws of the men. The strange octopus beings pulsated slowly, rising and down at leisure. They were perfectly balanced, resting their full, blubbery weight on the heads of the men.

Speechless at this new horror, the group stared at the figures as Daniel shot his light beam from one to the next and then right around the room to see whether any more creatures were hiding in the corners.

FEELING her way along the walls, Rachel made her way through the first cave. Her fingers met smooth surfaces mostly, although there were lots of little nicks and scratches marking them, every one of which she felt. Every so often, she encountered a deep groove that she enjoyed running her fingers down. She hummed to herself as she ambled through the pitch-black darkness, trying to keep the fear at bay.

One of her major anxieties was that she might step in something soft, a dead creature or some sort of deposit. If she thought about it for longer than a second, it made her stop or certainly prevented her from treading with any confidence. Fortunately, her path had been clear so far, and each of her steps had found solid ground. She hadn't even felt the splash of a single puddle.

Another fear was that there might be something waiting for her further on, perhaps at the centre of one of the caves. There was no way of knowing whether there were any of those leathery demon things standing there in the dark, waiting, although she sensed she might hear or smell them first before they attacked. She pushed this thought away, too, and kept going. Surely, she would find her way out eventually? The journey through the dark seemed endless.

The one thing that kept her going was the Dunamis. Somewhere deep in her gut, she was certain she was not alone. She could see herself in her mind's eye, looking down from a hundred feet above, a tiny figure wandering from one cave to another in the dark, blindly putting one foot in front of the other. But at the same time, her heart told her that the lover of her soul—that was how the Rescuer had described himself—was walking with her by her side. She knew she was safe, even in the dark.

While this made perfect sense to the white-haired Rachel, the black-haired Rachel of yesterday, who was totally afraid of the dark, would have scoffed and called the new Rachel "certifiable." "Everybody knows you're alone in the universe, and there's no meaning and no sense to life, you idiot," she would have told herself. "I mean, just look at the world. Stop living in fairyland and pull yourself back to reality."

Instead, this white-haired Rachel, this anti-Rachel, said, "Dunamis, lead me on. Keep me safe. Which way now?"

"This way," said the Dunamis somewhere deep inside her. "Okay then, let's go."

She kept on walking as one wall turned into another, connecting one cave to the next. Then, she felt a prompt to swap from one wall to the opposite one. She asked the Dunamis whether he was sure, took a deep breath, and turned.

It was a leap of faith to leave the wall she was clutching and spacewalk like an astronaut leaping away from the ship to fix an antenna while relying solely on her umbilical cables to keep her alive.

She spread her arms out to feel the way and crossed the room carefully, one step at a time. At length, she found the opposite wall and followed it in the same direction she had been travelling. It curved around and continued for a long distance, and her hands moved across the cold, hard face, feeling every bump and indentation.

As she walked, her mind started to play tricks on her. She could see images from her homeland: Griffton Cliff in the distance, seagulls over the city, Griffton's Central Plaza with the government buildings, and the square of grass with the sundial and the benches. Her mother's face shone in the sunlight.

But she knew it was completely dark, and there was nothing to see at all. They were just old ghosts of memories, the contents of the inside of her overheated mind. And perhaps that was all this world was—the contents of her mind, projected onto some strange reality. Maybe she was lying unconscious somewhere in a hospital bed, next to Iona, or dreaming in her room at 42 Russet Road, Griffton, while her dad sat in the living room, drinking whiskey and staring blankly at the TV.

"Help. Help me," called a voice from deeper into the cave system.

"If this is make-believe, then it sounds very realistic," Rachel told herself. She listened harder to determine where the voice was coming from, but it fell silent.

After pausing for a while, she plucked up the courage to call out, "Hello? I can hear you! I'm here. Are you okay?"

A voice that she knew came back to her. "Rachel? Is that you, Rachel? Rachel Race!"

THE CREATURES MADE a quiet slurping sound as they bobbed slowly up and down.

"They look like spiders," whispered Cameron.

Rory added, "Yeah. Big, fat, alien spiders."

Daniel stared, aghast, directing his flashlight toward the three men and the beings.

"That's Caleb," he gasped. "It really is him. If I'm not mistaken, these are Eli and Anton, Caleb's friends. Bella, keep your light on. I need to get something from my bag. I'm going to try and prise that thing off his head."

Daniel pulled out his penknife and extended the blade. Gripping it tightly, he approached the large, eyeless creature that had Caleb in its clutches. With determination, he pulled his arm back and stabbed hard into the body of the beast.

Arabella felt Micah jolt next to her, and she put her arm across his chest to keep him back. "It's all right, Micah. Look. Daniel's going to be fine."

Thick liquid oozed from the spider creature, dripping down Caleb's face as it tumbled forward, slumping to the ground with a grotesque splat. There was a thick stench in the air of rotting food. Rory covered his nose with his sleeve. "Pee-yeu!" he said. His high-pitched voice echoed around the cave.

Caleb began to stir, and Daniel quickly brought down the two other creatures with the skill of an assassin. Gutted, they landed on the ground and stayed still. Caleb, Anton, and Eli were free. Arabella could feel Micah getting more agitated. He started growling. "Micah, are you all right?"

Eli and Anton opened their eyes and groaned.

"Caleb!" Eli croaked, his voice hoarse, but Caleb stared blankly into space.

Suddenly, Micah let out a primal scream, startling everyone. He pushed Arabella aside and rushed over to the three men, giving Daniel a hard shove that almost knocked him off balance. Arabella's beam lit his form, and she saw he was holding two long knives, one in each hand.

"Micah, are you mad? Where did you get those from?" she cried out.

Micah emitted a bloodcurdling shriek and lunged towards Caleb.

Eli was quick, though, and placed himself between Micah and his friend. Meanwhile, Anton threw himself at Micah in order to topple him over. But it was all in vain.

Before they could do anything else to stop him, with a fierceness that surprised everyone, Micah plunged one of his blades into Anton and the other into Eli. The men roared and then fell silent. He left the blades buried deep in their bodies and loomed over Caleb with his bare hands, ready to grip his throat. Eli and Anton neither moved nor made any sound. They were dead.

"No!" screamed Daniel. "Stop, Micah!"

He threw himself bodily at Micah to prevent him from doing any more damage, dropping both his torch and his penknife in the move. He was successful in barging Micah into the cave wall, but as the light went away, Micah disappeared from view. Arabella started screaming, and the boys cried loudly. In the darkness, Micah laughed insanely.

Daniel located him by his laughter and hit his opponent in the chest. He hadn't had to fight anyone for a very long time but had lost none of his skills. He got a couple of sharp jabs into the assailant's rib cage, though he tripped over one of the dead men. However, it didn't stop the horrible laughter that came from his throat. Micah had become demented. Snarling, Daniel punched him to the ground.

Daniel wanted to finish him with a blow to the head or neck. But, at the same time, he thought that if something had taken him over, he shouldn't kill him in case he could save the lad. It felt like one of Samyaza's twisted tricks.

"Micah, I thought you were with us. How could you do this? What is wrong with you?" Daniel panted. He held tightly onto Micah's shoulders, pinning him down, anxiously glancing at the dead men in the shadows and Caleb, who sat stock-still.

Arabella turned the glare of her light on Micah and Daniel. They both watched in horror as he shape-shifted from being the young, beautiful eighteen-year-old whom they knew so well into an older, stockier man with a red face and grey, wispy hair. His pale skin faded away, withering like a leaf in a time-lapse photography film. His thick, dark, wavy hair shrank away and left behind a balding, freckled pate. Micah changed into someone else entirely before their very eyes.

"I bet you didn't see that coming," laughed Zed. "This is the way of the world, my friends. This is the way things happen here." Then he started singing, "One, two, three, four, five, once I caught a fish alive. Six, seven, eight, nine ten, then I let it go again."

"Shut up," Daniel screamed into his face. "You shut up!"

But Zed continued, "Why did you let it go? Because he grabbed my children so. Which children did he grab? The ones over there, you see, my children have your children now, and if you let me go, we'll let you go. You and yours, I mean." The man sneered.

"What?" Daniel fumbled for his torch, found it, and directed the beam toward his family. A group of six or seven odd-looking pale boys were holding Rory and Cameron hostage. The strange white boys all looked identical to each other and had their hands over the mouths of the Harcourt children. They looked like street urchins with bare feet, expressionless faces, and tight little fists.

"Decisions, decisions, Daniel. What to do?" sang Zed. "Quit

while you're ahead. That's my advice. Give up and go home. It's all over, anyways."

He pushed Daniel away and got up to his feet. He had red eyes and a maniacal grin.

"What have you done with Micah? The real Micah?"

"Who says I'm not the real Micah? I could be. I could have been Micah all along."

"Well, you're not. I'm guessing you are a servant of Samyaza."

"Ah, that I am. He is my master. He wants you to know the revolution has started, Daniel. The war has begun. Here and on the Earth. We are taking back this planet. Samyaza will prevail."

Zed broke free of Daniel's grasp and scampered over to the dead men. He pulled out the long blade from the man in the middle, who was slumped over dead, and held it out towards Caleb.

"Your turn," he spat.

But Caleb woke from his stupor. He reacted fast, reaching for Daniel's blade, the penknife that was lying on the ground before him. He grasped it tightly and brought it upwards in a swinging motion, sticking it hard into the underside of Zed's arm. Zed cried out in pain.

Caleb got to his feet as Daniel appeared behind Zed, grabbed him by the shoulders, and threw him against the cave wall. Meanwhile, Arabella broke the boys free from the alien family, and somehow, with many kicks and shoves, they were able to escape and scramble over to Daniel.

Daniel grabbed Caleb's hand and pulled him to his feet. The Harcourt family gathered together and pulled each other out of the cave and through the interconnected caverns. They left the other two bodies behind.

Zed and the boys let them go and didn't pursue them. But they heard Zed's voice following them through the caves.

"Go on and run. It's been fun, an enjoyable way to pass the

time, but I have work to do now. So go, my enemies, followers of the Rescue-no one and his Duna-missed again! Off you go."

Daniel and Arabella guided the stupefied Caleb between them, with the children by their side. With Daniel pointing the beam in front of them, they stumbled from one cave to another, trying to retrace their steps.

None of it looked familiar to any of them, and they walked for a long time, escaping by degrees from Zed and his boys.

With heavy steps and tired children who were silenced by their ordeal, the group finally emerged into the red daylight of another mezzanine world afternoon. The scene outside was unfamiliar. Instead of the hostile valley, with its cracks and chasms, they could see streams of water and, in the distance, fields full of long, lush grass.

CHAPTER 18

It was Micah, as she'd hoped, and he'd been tied up and left in the caves. She knew him from his voice and had caressed his face and cheeks with her bare hands in the dark. She knew for sure it was him. It was unmistakably his distinctive jawline and wavy hair. He gestured to his wrists and feet, showing that he had been bound tightly. Rachel, acting quickly, set to work. Tugging and untying the knots, she managed to free him from the coarse twine that had held him captive. He looked at her with gratitude, rubbing his wrists as the tension left his body.

"I must admit, I did wonder if I'd ever get out of here. They jumped me. I was in the cave, looking for the boys. Some people grabbed me and tied me up. It was so dark, though. I couldn't see who they were."

"Is the family okay? How are the boys and Arabella?"

"I don't know, Rachel. They moved on. They left me behind. I don't know why, but I'm sure they had their reasons," said Micah sadly. He added, "Let's hope they didn't get attacked as well, though I think Daniel can look after himself when it comes to trouble."

"I'm sure you're right. Well, maybe they're not too far away. How long ago do you think it was they moved on?"

"I don't know. It was a while ago."

"We should get moving then. Maybe we can find them. After all, I found you."

Rachel finished untying Micah and helped him to his feet. He held onto her tightly in the dark, which she liked. "Listen to me feeling sorry for myself," he said. "How are you, Rachel? Have you been okay since you came in? I know we left you there on Griffton Cliff, but we didn't see you come through the head. We didn't know for sure whether you made it, but I hoped you did. We've been looking for you ever since. We never stopped."

"I'm absolutely fine."

"I mean, we hung around for a while to see if you followed us. We also wanted to know if those men came through, but they didn't."

"I'm okay, Micah. Better than okay. You don't need to worry about me. In fact, I've had an adventure. It's been scary at times and amazing, too, but I'll tell you all about it later. Come on, let's get moving. I think I know how to get back out the way I came. It isn't too far."

THEY SAT ON THE ROCKS, Daniel, Arabella, Caleb, and the boys. The youngsters had recovered quickly from their ordeal. They were paddling in the stream and looking for fish, or at least anything that resembled fish. Every so often, a squeal of delight could be heard, which was at odds with what had just happened in the caves.

Daniel and Arabella had their arms around Caleb, their dear friend. He sat quietly and stared across the stream with haunted eyes. He still looked and felt muscular, but he'd lost weight and looked like a shadow of the Caleb they knew and loved.

He took the news about his friends Eli and Anton in stony silence, not reacting when Daniel suggested they go back and look for their bodies and perhaps bring them out and give them a proper burial. He just shook his head and said, "No. We leave them in there. They're gone. It's over. Let the caves be their tomb."

Around their heads, a handful of tiny bubble creatures floated, delicate frogs in spherical casings that moved leisurely through the air. The breeze blew softly and joined with the sound of the rippling stream to create a smooth musical score as Caleb convalesced.

All the while, the blood-red sun shone down, tainting the sky with its strange rays. Puffy magenta clouds hung like overweight gods high over the figures' heads. Further downstream, half a dozen boulders floated in mid-air.

Suddenly, Cameron called out, from where he was crouching on the rocks in the stream, "Hey, it's our friends!"

"Who?" asked Daniel in a daze.

"Rachel! And Micah! Is that you, Micah, this time? Or are you that other guy?" shouted Rory. "The bad one?"

In the distance, two figures emerged from another cave entrance. They walked slowly, falteringly, holding onto each other. Rachel looked the stronger of the two. The Harcourt family watched them trace the line of the rocky wall and move nearer to them.

From time to time, Rachel put her hand out to support them against the solid wall of the cave. Micah rubbed his wrists, and Arabella saw Micah didn't have a cut on his head like the other one. She shared her observations with the others.

"It is Micah! Micah and Rachel, it's so good to see you," she called.

Daniel said quickly, "Are you sure it's really them?"

Arabella stood up and stared, her arms by her side. After a while, she said, "It's definitely them. This isn't a trick. Although, look at her hair. She looks so different. What do you think happened?"

Her question hung in the air.

Minutes later, they embraced their friends, checked them for cuts and bruises, and chattered away. The boys commented on Rachel's new hair colour, and everyone wanted to have a look at Micah's wrists and ankles to check he was in one piece. Having got both Rachel and Micah talking, Daniel was finally convinced they were the real deal. He began to relax at last.

Caleb was the only one who sat alone on the rocks, his hooded eyes staring into space. Like a slab of solid stone himself, his torso was hunched forward at an angle, with his arms resting on his knees. And so he sat, still as a mountain, tormented by his private world.

As NIGHT DREW NEAR, the group shared stories, except for Caleb, who stayed quiet and seemed content to listen, though he furrowed his brow from time to time. Daniel asked what had happened to him, but he had no intention of sharing the story. He mumbled something vague about Bolivia and gave a slight shrug, indicating he preferred to be left alone with his thoughts. His eyes drifted away, clearly not ready to relive whatever ordeal he had endured.

They listened intently as Rachel told them about Zed, also known as Zaelaza, the shape-shifter who had drugged her with tea in his house on the black-rock plateau. The revelation that he had gone on to kill Caleb's friends horrified them all. As Rachel recounted the events, they wondered about the strange albino boy, whom she identified as Olm. She explained he was a Spawner, meaning he could exist as one or multiple versions of himself, each of them looking exactly alike. The boys shuddered, remembering how the Olm brothers had seized them, holding them prisoner with eerie precision.

She told them about her incredible encounter with the Rescuer and how his fire had overwhelmed her and his face had blazed like the sun. She explained, as best she could, how her hair had turned white, and her father had fallen into this world and was somewhere out there. Excitedly, she talked about hearing the voice of the Dunamis and knowing she was not alone. Daniel and Arabella grinned and nodded, their eyes wet with tears. None of it seemed to shock or surprise them or Micah.

Also, with tears, Cameron told her about the chessboard in the scrubby desert that had swallowed his foot but that Micah had worked out how to unlock it with coloured crystals and set him free. Rachel smiled and raised her eyebrows as he told her his animated story.

She, in turn, told them about the scary leopard that chased her but rolled over in the end, the black demon, and the white angel who rescued her. She pointed out the body of the dead creature over in the distance, but nobody was in a hurry to see. They listened as she described her two new weapons of laughter coupled with faith in the Rescuer and his Dunamis. But she stopped as she noticed Caleb was shaking his head sadly. He had listened intently to a point but was evidently finding it difficult now.

"Is everything okay, Caleb, my brother?" Daniel enquired of him.

In a gruff voice, he snapped, "Dreams and illusions. That's all it is."

"I'm sorry?" asked Rachel.

"There is no Dunamis, and there is definitely no Rescuer. Sorry to disappoint you, folks. I know that now."

"What do you mean? Are you feeling okay?" Daniel shot back. "Yes, Daniel, I'm finally in my right, rational mind, and I can see clearly now. My eyes are open. Wide open."

"Did you hear anything I said?" asked Rachel indignantly.

"Yes, I was listening," replied Caleb in a low voice. Then, looking towards the caves, he said, "I was mistaken. We were all mistaken. When my wife Rosemary died, there was no rescue for her or me."

"What do you mean?" asked Daniel.

"What I mean is that I need to sleep now. I'm tired. I'm so tired, Daniel. Weary to the point of death." He grinned a grim and humourless smile and bowed his head slightly, the weight of his expression heavy with unspoken intent.

"Are you telling me, Caleb Noble, the man who introduced me to the Dunamis and a life free of Samyaza, that you were mistaken? Have you lost your mind?"

"No, my friend. I have perfect clarity now. There is no Rescuer. There's no Dunamis and no Creator. I wish there were. In some way, it would be quite comforting. We'd all have a crutch to help us hobble along through our wretched lives until we die. But there you have it."

"No!" Rachel said emphatically. "My Rescuer is alive! I know because I met him! I know him. And because he's alive, that means I'm alive, more alive than I've ever been. I mean, look at my hair! Do you think it was this colour before I met him?"

Caleb shrugged but didn't look up.

Daniel added, "What about the miracles? You told me about the healing you did through the Dunamis across the world. What about Romania, Bali, and France? You called on the Dunamis, and he had compassion for people and healed them. You told me that you frequently hear things about people—things that are true and things that come true. You have knowledge of details and events! You told me that in Indonesia, you spoke a foreign language as though it were your own tongue and again in Slovakia in the mountains. You told me these things, Caleb, and many more stories like them. You and no one else. You've lived them, and I have found them to be true myself."

"I was deluded. I was mistaken. Dreams and illusions, nothing more."

Rachel chimed in, "I was trapped in that horrible cell on

Griffton Cliff. You knew where I was, and you pulled the door off its hinges and rescued me and Lake. Don't you remember? You introduced us to the Dunamis, and we met him! I've had dreams of the Rescuer. And I know him, and he loves me, even though I'm not like him—clean and perfect. I'm me, and he loves me just as I am, with all my faults and weaknesses. He listens to me. He is real, Caleb! And you know him better than we do."

"No. I have been mistaken, deluded. Maybe I wanted it to be the case, but it's not."

"No, Caleb, you're mistaken now!" insisted Daniel. "You taught me everything. Everything about the Creator, the Rescuer, and his Dunamis, and I know them now for myself. What about the time I died, Caleb? What about that? You were passing by in a boat. Was that just a coincidence? You told me you saw it happen before it did, like in a vision, and you jumped into the water and found me. You and Eli brought me back to life, for goodness' sake!"

"Coinci…" Caleb began slowly.

"There can be no coincidences! There's no room for coincidences," Daniel exploded. "These things all happened, Caleb. There are no other explanations other than what we are all saying separately."

Caleb shook his head and was quiet for several minutes. At last, he said, "You were never dead, Daniel. You were unconscious. Beyond that, I don't really know."

Daniel wandered deep into his own thoughts, and Arabella stared at the children.

Rachel sat weeping in her hands, wrestling with what she had seen and come to believe. Through her fingers, she could see long strands of thick white hair that used to be jet black. A year and a half ago, she had paid to get blue streaks put into her black hair, and eventually, these had grown out and left her with her natural colour.

She stared at the long white tresses between her fingers and sobbed.

CHAPTER 19

Jia Li's family hails from Chengdu, in Sichuan Province, but she lived in a small village nestled in the mountains northwest of the city.

She recited one of her favourite poems, 'I Stand Alone,' by the Tang Dynasty poet Du Fu, who lived in Chengdu around the year seven hundred and sixty.

"A falcon hovers at the edge of the sky. Two gulls drift slowly up the river," she said in her tiny voice, speaking into the wind.

"Vulnerable while they ride the wind, they coast and glide with ease. Dew is heavy on the grass below; the spider's web is ready. Heaven's ways include the human: among a thousand sorrows, I stand alone."

She stood watching Singing Lake, far beneath her village, a treacherous drop below. Its surface glittered, silvery-white, like liquid metal shimmering at the bottom of the deep gorge. Jagged mountain walls rose on either side, framing the lake in a still, profound silence. The sheer vastness of the scene filled her with awe, the quiet adding to the mystery of the shimmering waters.

One year, she was fortunate to visit Du Fu's house, where he wrote many of his poems, including 'My Thatched Hut was

Torn Apart by Autumn Wind.' In general, though, she didn't get across to the city very often. She didn't really want to, mainly because of the bad memories but also because there were so many people living in the city, and it made her head hurt.

Sichuan Province had millions of people living in it, and too many of them lived in Chengdu. Chengdu and East Sichuan were noisy, smelly, dirty, and crowded, crammed with cars and shoe factories. Where she lived, life was quite different. It was another kingdom altogether, a magical kingdom. She lived at the edge of the world in a place with huge mountains that rose to twenty-five thousand feet.

Stony farms sat on terraced hills, linked by rough roads and steep slopes. The mountains in West Sichuan hid dense bamboo forests, home to wild pandas and secret monsters. There were swamps and hidden dangers with a long, twisting road to Tibet that took two weeks to travel by truck.

Three years ago, when she was thirteen, she had joined a village of tough teenagers who had been abandoned by their families for various reasons. In her case, she had been accused of stealing gold, and the shame of her family was intense. It had been untrue, a lie created by enemies of her father, and she had been the scapegoat. She didn't like to think about it because when she thought about her parents, her body hurt too much.

It was her turn to cook for her community tonight, and she was planning something spicy and warm to go with the noodles. The evenings were growing cooler, which was partly to do with the change in season and partly to do with the altitude.

As she prepared to go back inside, she noticed a tiny dot in the sky descending from the high mountains descending at a sharp forty-five-degree angle. It had a broad wingspan and quickly covered a vast distance, gliding effortlessly through the air.

Soon, the bird—an eagle, she presumed—was parallel with her balcony, though still too far to make out clearly. Jia Li squinted into the distance, narrowing her big, round eyes into two long slits. Her long, black hair framed her face, elongating its already graceful oval shape as she focused intently on the distant figure.

As it came into view, Jia Li quickly realised it wasn't like any bird she had ever seen. Instead, it looked more like an evil creature; its thick skin, black head, and body gave it an unnatural appearance. It resembled a bat more than a bird, and the way it was homing in on her made her uneasy. Her heart quickened as she thought she glimpsed fangs in its open mouth.

In no time at all, the dark figure was on her balcony. Not wanting to take any chances, Jia Li chopped at the animal with the side of her hand. It gave out a high-pitched shriek as it tumbled off the balcony rail. She felt guilty, but it had been a reflexive reaction.

It popped back up and came at her. Alarmed, she ran into the house and pulled the door shut.

"Ri, help! There's a monster outside!" Jia Li called out to Ri, the leader of her community. The small kitchen window shattered as the leathery creature entered the room. Glass bathed the floor. The monster, which Jia Li could now see, was both leathery and furry, like some grotesque mix of a bat and a monkey, plopped on the old wooden table. Its weight made the wood creak, and its piercing gaze locked onto her. It was clear the creature wanted her full attention.

Ri must have been out of earshot, so Jia Li called again and then shouted for help from anyone. The creature hissed at her, staring through small beady eyes. She grabbed a pan from the side of the stove. It was a solid-base metal pan that she was going to use to toss the vegetables in.

The unwelcome visitor spread its wings and dove at her, aiming for one of her hands. Reacting quickly, Jia Li swung her pan with force, making a satisfying thud. There was another thud as the creature connected with the kitchen wall.

Jia Li grinned. She picked up a large kitchen knife and went over to where it lay, unmoving, by the wall. She kicked it gently with her foot to see if it was dead.

The thing reared up again, still full of fight. It hopped once, then launched itself at her with renewed fury. With a gasp, she slashed at the animal and caught it on the side of its body. The knife made a nick, barely slowing it down. Before she could bring the knife back up again, the bat closed in one last time and attached its sharp teeth around the lower part of her thumb.

In searing pain, Jia Li tried to slash at the monster with the knife in her right hand, but the agony clouded her aim. Blood spilled from her wound, and in her panic, she dropped the knife. She could only watch in horror as the bat creature hopped onto the window ledge, leaped over the jagged glass, and soared into the sky, a piece of her thumb clenched between its jaws. It faltered in its path a couple of times as it flew, wavering in the air, but soon rose out of sight.

Jia Li looked at her thumb and screamed at the top of her lungs. Ri and the others finally appeared and came to her aid, witnessing the blood on her hands, her wrist, and the kitchen floor.

12345

The excitement of having the Dream Fighters around had worn off after about a week. José was in one of his dark moods today, and it was clear to Diego that he was getting restless and bored.

"Do you ever think about running away?" asked José.

"I like it here, brother. You know, my family is here and everything."

"I think about running away. I think about it all the time."

"Perhaps at the weekend, we can have an adventure?"

José grinned at his younger brother. Carlos and Sergio, their older brothers, were working further up in the fields. To start with, they had enjoyed being Dream Fighter warriors, being trained in hand-to-hand combat, both with and without swords.

It was also fun to go into the local village and cause trouble, knowing they would win in any fight. It was hilarious to see the faces of their friends, particularly Gerardo, who lived on the big farm next door.

In addition, their father seemed prouder than ever of them, laughing as they wrestled and fought. The farm was running smoothly again. The Americans were no longer threatening them, as their saviours had promised, and life was good in general.

But from time to time, the Dream Fighters bothered the girls, and they were always eating, smoking, drinking beer, and strutting around. Sometimes, they pushed the boys around and were rough with them, which was not okay with José.

In many ways, life was just like it was before they had arrived: hard work for long hours and only football for entertainment, which the Dream Fighters were not interested in. Their dad would fall asleep with the paper in his lap, and the days would pass by. Every so often, José wondered if they were waiting for something to happen. Nobody told him anything.

"Adventures are good. But one day, I'm going to leave Bolivia and see the world," he said.

THE DREAM FIGHTERS weren't great conversationalists, but Kumiko was okay with that. She had a lot to do anyway: phone calls, planning, logistics, and organising things and, more recently, TV and radio work across the country.

What was starting to annoy her was that they were leaving their stuff all over the mansion! She was the only one doing any work at the moment, although she knew that would change soon. These hefty warriors would be called upon imminently to assist the city and make it better than before.

There were a few dozen warriors in the house at the moment, big men who kept themselves to themselves and stayed out of her way as best they could. They relaxed by fighting or arm wrestling at a table or doing their archery out in the garden. They had also built an assault course outside just for kicks.

When they weren't doing combat drills, they were drinking and baiting each other in the rooms that they had claimed as their quarters. Every morning and evening, they would go off down to the basement and do their chanting and rituals in order to connect with Samyaza.

Kumiko sometimes went with them, just to see the black cloud descend with the sparkling lights in it and a sense of his dark presence with them. But she was glad she wasn't required to do any of that herself. She was a special case, fortunate to have a direct line to Samyaza, and they knew she was worthy of the utmost respect because of this.

When she wasn't working, she'd help herself to a bottle of champagne, switch on the big plasma screen, and watch one of the hundreds of films on the shelf. Or she would take a long and luxurious shower in the ensuite that was attached to the master bedroom. It was so nice to wash the city out of her hair: the dust from the rubble and the continual stench of burning. The hot jets would come down, cascading across her flesh, and the aroma of lavender body wash would rise as her melodic rock music took flight in the background. It was luxurious.

However, she didn't get to relax as much as she liked. After all, there was work to do, and creating and managing chaos took careful planning and was a time-consuming exercise.

The phone call she was about to take was an example of this. "It's Kumiko."

"Ah, yes. I wanted to talk to you," said the woman on the other end of the line, the publishing director at the Griffton News. She had a New England accent, Anglicised from living in Britain for the past decade.

"So talk." Kumiko sat back in her leather chair and swung

her long legs onto the hardwood desk as she often did when she was getting into a call.

"First of all, I am obviously delighted with all the news stories you guys are creating for our paper. Sales have doubled. That was as I expected and what we agreed."

"Glad you're delighted," said Kumi.

"But what I am not happy with is that you have taken my news editor. I want him back. This was not part of our agreement. Is he safe? Is he even alive? Why have you taken him?"

"So many questions. I thought I made it clear at our last meeting that there were many things the partners wouldn't understand and many things I can't tell you at this stage. You need to do your job, and let me do mine."

"I don't understand the rationale of how you operate."

"You will get your payday, rest assured. But our methods are unconventional because the prize is so great. There will be casualties. We made that clear at the outset, but Samyaza will prevail."

"I'm not in this for your Mr Samyaza. I just want what's coming to me."

"Oh, you will get what's coming to you."

"Is that a threat, young girl?"

"Just read your small print, Janet. Somewhere in the contract, you will see that our methods are covered in the agreement."

"Ah, the contract. I see. Well, I want to note that I am not happy."

"Just sit tight. Your part of the arrangement is being secured as we speak, but you must understand that things take time. Good things come to she who waits."

"Very well then. But is there any way of getting my news editor back? He's one of the best I've seen in all my years in the industry."

"You sure he can't be replaced by someone else?"

"He creates a good product. He knows how to get the best

out of the writers. He's good at his job. What more can I say? Beyond that, I have no personal affection for him."

"It's not really how we work here, but I'll see what I can do," said Kumi. "What's his name? Let me make a note. I'll see if we can still locate him."

"Michael Wright, but they call him Mike."

CHAPTER 20

Daniel, Micah, Arabella, and Rachel left the boys to chatter with each other and play in the stream near Caleb. He reclined on the bank at the water's edge and closed his eyes. He seemed content to lie there, staying quiet and exploring his thoughts.

It was almost night-time now, though the figures could still just about see each other under the glow of the reddish sky. They decided to get some rest and decide in the morning about where to go next.

"He really isn't himself," said Daniel.

"I know," said Micah, sadly.

"Maybe he will snap out of it," Rachel added.

"He's been through a lot," Arabella noted. "I expect he just needs some time to get over things."

"Those things we saw, the creatures that rested on his head and on the heads of his friends, I am sure they're responsible for the change," said Daniel.

"What were they like?" asked Rachel.

"Horrible. They were horrible, like bloated spiders, feeding," explained Arabella.

"It's certainly like nothing I've ever seen before, and Samyaza showed me a lot of things. It was like the only purpose of these things was to suck the life off Caleb, Eli, and Anton. Those poor men."

"I suggest we rest here for the night and take turns to keep watch. That's what we've been doing, Rachel, not that we've come across any trouble during the nights. But even though our bodies are different in this world, it feels good to rest, wouldn't you agree?"

"Yes, I don't get hungry, but I sometimes need to sit down or sleep, and I enjoy the way things feel, like water on my feet or the breeze on my face. It really is a funny land. It's so much like home but so different."

"Well, that's a plan then. Let's talk again in the morning and see if we can get some direction from the Dunamis," concluded Daniel.

"So, he does really exist?" Rachel asked.

"Never doubt it," he replied.

In the morning, a tall figure was waiting patiently for them as the red sun came up. Despite being a land where humans didn't need to sleep, the group certainly felt like they had had a good night's slumber. Blearily, Rachel opened her eyes and stared at the man. It looked at first as though his white robes were made of lightning, flashing and sparkling with sudden bursts of energy. Then, they settled down and became white.

"I know you. You're the one who saved me from that monster. You're Megatron."

The angel smiled and said in a musical voice, "Yes, I am Mattatron. I've been sent to help you. All of you."

The others looked in awe at the being, with the boys exclaiming out loud. Only Caleb stayed asleep, or at least unmoving. Arabella bowed down before the angel, but he said to her kindly, "Oh no, don't do that. I am your servant, not your master. We are different from you and live in the presence of the Creator, yes, but it's you he made in his image, and he loves you as children. As for us, we live to serve him and also you. So do not bow before me unless you do so to recognise the Rescuer's worth, in which case I will join you."

"Oh boy, a real-life angel," said Rory. "Wait until I get back and tell my class! They're never going to believe me."

"This is really cool. Can you fly?" asked Cameron.

"Yes, young man. I can fly." He showed them his powerful wings, yet appeared light, and they gasped and cooed. With his wings outstretched and standing tall in his white clothes, he resembled a star, bright and magnificent.

By now, Caleb was paying some attention but was sitting grumpily with his arms around his knees. The angel addressed him.

"Caleb, I need to take you on a quick journey. Will you come with me?"

Caleb rubbed his palm on his short-cropped grey hair and sniffed. He stared over the stream at the caves without blinking.

"Caleb, the Rescuer knows you have walked closely with him and that you are weary now. He would like to talk face to face."

Caleb looked directly at the angel. "You know, I met one of your kind not long ago. It was the first time for me. I met him in New York City. I was with Serena. Do you happen to know how she is?"

The angel paused for thought. Then he said, "No, I don't know how she is. Will you come with me?" he asked Caleb again.

"I will come with you."

"Very good. For the rest of you, we have laid out some food and drinks. Don't be afraid; we have taken the body of the beast. All is safe here for now. Eat, relax, and wait for my return. I will tell you more then."

The angel picked Caleb up in his muscular arms, spread his wings, and flew above their heads and over the caves, leaving them gawping at each other or staring up at the rocky ridge.

As they rose above the caves, he marvelled at the fact that he was being taken for a ride by a real-life angelic being, expecting this reality to merge into another horrific nightmare. After all, he had been forced to find a home in those sinister and cruel scenarios that twisted his memories into sadistic weapons aimed at his heart.

He saw Daniel, Arabella, Rachel, and the boys recede swiftly into the distance, staring up at him with their mouths open. The stream unfolded before him and shrank as he ascended. Soon, Caleb was enjoying the feeling of flight, particularly flying without an aircraft. Now he knew what it felt like to be a bird.

Caleb gazed around him, catching his breath. Down below, he caught sight of rocks and ravines, bizarre plant life, and land formations he had never seen before. He glimpsed a chequer-board of fiery stones, a field of dark-red rocks, and a circle of pale, beige monoliths.

In the dark stasis that was his time in the caves, he was used to his mind moving from one scenario to another, all of them degenerating in the end. During that experience, he felt like his mind and heart had broken.

However, feeling the air on his face and in his lungs again and seeing the incredible scenery around him, he started to experience a new feeling: hope. But he fought this feeling, knowing in his heart that he had been utterly betrayed, tortured, and abandoned. Worse than this, his loved ones were all dead: first Rosemary, then Eli and Anton, and possibly even Serena. He could not cope with living life alone. It was more than he could bear.

After a while, they came to an opening, and Mattatron took them down into a cylindrical red-rock canyon. As they landed on the sandy ground, Caleb looked up at the red and sand-coloured layers that suggested that water had once rushed through the rocks, eroding the walls and leaving beautiful horizontal lines. The place smelt dusty and ancient and was formed of several curved columns that rose into the air.

The angel released him and stepped back, and Caleb stood and stretched to his full height, raising his arms into the air and spreading his fingers. He was still wearing a tight black T-shirt over his brawny frame, and his round shoulder muscles bulged as he lifted his arms. Mattatron stood nearby, several feet taller than Caleb and as wide as a gate.

Powdery sunlight filtered through the hole at the top of the canyon and bathed both of the figures in a reddish glow.

As they stood and waited, they heard quiet footsteps approaching. Caleb watched as the Rescuer walked around the corner of a column of rock and into the clearing. His eyes widened. The Rescuer was tall and battle-hardened, with a youthful face and bright eyes that put him in his mid-thirties. A white platinum crown was pressed onto his long white hair, and he wore a bright white tunic.

As the Rescuer strode towards him, Caleb's gaze fell on a black tattoo running down one of the man's thighs. The letters were long and bold, etched in a language Caleb couldn't decipher. The unfamiliar script seemed heavy with meaning, though its significance was lost on him.

A sudden rage gripped Caleb's heart, and he put his head down and rushed at the King, swinging his fist. "I hate you! I hate you!" he yelled at full volume. His punch landed on the Rescuer's brawny chest, but he stood tall and took another couple of blows as Caleb roared in his face.

The Rescuer took a last punch and then held him close. Caleb wept.

"I gave everything to you. I loved you with all my heart, my soul and strength. I don't understand. Why? Why, my king?"

Caleb sobbed. "Why me? Why did you choose me? Why did you make my life so hard?"

Caleb crumpled to the ground, and the Rescuer bowed low and held him in his arms.

Then he sat down and cradled Caleb's head at his breast. The angel also sat down and rested against the high wall of the narrow canyon. Caleb felt the familiar presence of the Dunamis surrounding him, comforting him and strengthening him. His eyes were closed, and he felt the arms of the King around him. His heart and mind grew still, his opposition draining away.

"I'm sorry, my Master," Caleb sighed.

Time passed. Eventually, the Rescuer spoke through the Dunamis. His mouth stayed still, but the words formed inside Caleb's heart, as they had done so many times before.

"Grieve your friends but not as the world does. Know that I love Anton and Eli and also Rosemary. They are with me now. And I am with you, and you are in me, so be comforted, though the days are evil."

Then the Rescuer said in a low and gentle voice, "You are a straightforward and plain-speaking man, Caleb. In you, there is nothing false. So, I will tell you plainly. The enemy tested you and tested you hard. But what the enemy meant for evil, I have used it for good.

"You have endured much heartache and agony, with which I am not unfamiliar myself. But know that I am building strong character in you because you have responsibilities ahead. My ways are not yours, and I know they raise many questions in you, but still, you must trust. This is your burden and your strength to hold firm on the side of the mountain or in the sands of the desert. There are times when silence has the loudest voice, but I am with you in those times."

Caleb sighed but felt the warmth of the Dunamis, a warm fire in his veins. He had the impression he had been on the point of death, but the Dunamis had poured life back into him.

He continued, "I have more work for you to do, work that I

planned for you before the world began. You will see even greater things than you have seen thus far and have even greater adventures before your end comes. You are a man made for adventure, the slopes of the mountains and the depths of the desert, are you not?"

"I am," grinned Caleb weakly.

"You are built for a life lived to the full, charging ahead with the sun in your eyes and the wind at your back. You are my Caleb, a mighty warrior, a speaker of truth, and a man of strength, are you not?" asked the Rescuer assertively.

"I am," said Caleb, sitting up.

"You are a traveller, an encourager, a hero for many, my arms and my legs, an oasis of peace. You are my Caleb, are you not?"

"I am," Caleb said confidently. "I am your Caleb, my Rescuer, my King." Caleb stood to his feet, and so did the Rescuer and the angel.

"Yes, you are, and I love you with an everlasting love, always have, always will. Now, are you ready?"

"I'm ready, my King." In his mind, he said, "Rescuer, you are my strength and my joy, the reason I live and the reason I breathe. Your presence is all I seek. In your presence, I'm complete."

The Rescuer heard him and said, "What you say is true."

Caleb gazed at the face of his master.

"It's time for my angel to take you back now. Follow my Dunamis, and be of good cheer, Caleb."

The Rescuer walked unhurriedly away, around the corner of the big rock column that rose into the sky.

Caleb smiled at Mattatron and nodded. With nothing further said, the massive angel grabbed him to his chest, and they soared into the air and out through the top of the canyon.

CHAPTER 21

Word spread quickly across the Griffton News Tower like a squirrel running across a field, scurrying up the trunk of a tree, then leaping from branch to branch.

It started at reception as soon as the arrival came. Gabrielle communicated this to her friend in human resources via telephone. She sent a text to her boyfriend in accounts, and he sent out a Facebook message to his friends in various parts of the building, one of whom was Hayley, the news reporter on Lake's team.

Hayley let out a scream, which got the attention of the entire office. "Spike's back!" she yelled.

This was the first time any of the abductees had been found or returned. Many search parties had been sent out, but none of them had come up with the goods.

Lake leapt up. He had been writing yet another tragic story of a family torn apart by the recent violence. This one was a shopkeeper who had lost his livelihood and a family member when his store was burned down one night by mindless hoods.

Looking around the room, he said, "Where is he? Is he here?"

"Downstairs. He's downstairs, but he's coming up right now." Out in the corridor, the lift opened, and the thickset figure of Mike Wright shuffled out and appeared at the door of the newsroom. He looked at them happily with his laughter lines and thinning hair. Lake could see he was roughed up, with bruises on his cheek and forehead. He lowered his eyes when he saw the commotion, most likely expecting a quiet entrance. But instead, he walked modestly into a round of rapturous applause and hugs from some of the reporters. It was a hero's welcome.

"It's okay. Don't make a fuss. I'm fine."

Don came over and patted him on the back, grinning through his teeth and staring at him through his thick black glasses with a tear in his eye.

After he had allowed people to express their feelings fully, he ordered a meeting in the back room as usual. But this time, it was he who was the subject of the story. He said he'd try to give them answers to whatever questions they wanted to ask him, though he knew little.

After everyone had assembled in the meeting room, Mike said, "Shall we assume this is story one, people? Unless you guys think there's a more important story for today? Maybe there is; I haven't checked the news today."

"Oh, no. No, this is definitely story one, Mike," said Don, rolling up his sleeves and grinning as he revealed his hairy arms.

"Harvey, I'd like you to do this story. It's going to be a front page, your first, right?" said Mike.

Dark-haired Harvey smiled a huge smile and sat tall in his chair. "Yes, thanks, Mike."

"But don't get too smug. You still have to do a decent job of it."

"Oh, I will. I won't let you down," said Harvey quickly.

"I'm sure. Lake, will you help him if he needs it?"

Lake nodded on the other side of the table, with his tongue wedged into his cheek. "Sure, no problem. I'll babysit Harvey."

"Good then. I know you all have questions. After all, you're my journalists. First of all, I want you to know that I'm fine. So, Don, Harvey, Lake, Monica, Hayley, and the rest of you, shoot."

The impromptu press conference began. Harvey asked how Mike got taken.

"There was a knock at my door as I was about to leave for work. It was early, as you all know, I come in early. It was classic, really. I didn't get to see their faces apart from seeing a couple of guys built like brick outhouses. So anyway, they put a bag over my head and bundled me into a car. It was as quick as that."

"Who were they?" This came from Don, who added, "Or rather, who did they say they were?"

"They didn't say much. No demands and no explanations. Except they claimed they were people who followed someone called the Rescuer. They didn't say much else."

"Where did they take you?" Monica asked next.

"It was hard to tell, but we drove for about an hour, maybe, which tells me it was either over towards Polcombe or the other way, out east, or else north of the cliff."

Lake asked, "Did they hurt you?"

"Not really. They punched me a bit to start with, but I could tell their heart wasn't really in it. I used to do some boxing, you see. I can take a punch. No, they didn't really bother about us much. They kept us in separate cells, some sort of underground military facility. Maybe that's worth checking out.

"Anyway, I knew there were other people, though I couldn't see them. I talked to a few of them: a female lawyer, a head teacher, and a businessman. I'll give you their names and what I know about them in a bit so we can try to contact their families. We should do that as soon as we can."

"How long did they keep you?"

"Come on. You can work that one out, Harvey. You know when I went missing?"

"What did you do during the day?"

"Pace around mostly. Exercise a bit. Read novels. Talk to the other prisoners. They gave us food. We didn't starve."

"Why did they let you go?" Harvey enquired.

Mike gave a heavy sigh and stared at the desk. "I don't know, Harvey. I have no idea why they let me go. Why snatch a news editor in the first place? Maybe they wanted me to publish the story."

KUMIKO LAUGHED to herself as her driver took her down from the big house and into Griffton. The plan was working like a dream, and Samyaza had given her great power. If she took a dislike to somebody, all she needed to do was point her finger, and the mob would rush in and intervene. If she needed to exert more pressure, the Dream Fighters were at her beck and call to move in and take control of the situation, using whatever force was necessary.

The carnage had created enough mayhem to warrant a problem in need of a solution. With the attacks and the disappearances, the fear in Griffton was palpable. She was recognised wherever she went and hailed as the city's heroine, but because of her newfound fame, she travelled with bodyguards now. They were two towering Dream Fighter warriors in full armour, carrying swords and guns. It was a thrill, she thought.

As they drove towards the city centre, Kumiko saw groups of Dream Fighters policing the streets. She was proud of them, her army of peacekeepers, and there was plenty of work for them to do, keeping order, antagonising wannabe gangsters, and killing miscreants. With the police out of the way and the city leaders on her payroll, empire-building had never been so easy.

A couple of days ago, Samyaza had allowed her to see what the Dream Fighters looked like to him in the spiritual realm: black-hearted killers driven by dark spirits who rode on their backs. Each demon billowed like a cloak as they clung tightly onto the Dream Fighter's shoulders and bellowed murder into their minds.

She was impressed by the vision but said to him, "And what do I look like to you?"

"To me, you are beautiful," said her surfer boy, winking at her in her mind's eye.

"You charmer," she said.

"I think it's time to draw your Lake Emerson a little closer. I'm confident we're winning on the other side, but still, I sense that things aren't quite going to plan. Why don't you give him a call and offer him a job?"

"Good idea. Is it okay to take him back to the house?"

"Yes, of course. Try your best to get him onside, but if he snoops around too much or tries to oppose us, then you're going to need to kill him."

"What, myself?"

"If you like. Or you could get your bodyguards to do it."

"I'll give him a call."

12345

As Zed sat relaxing in his chair, staring into space, the Calloskira skulked quietly into his dingy wooden house on the rock. The furry creature had the Chinese girl's thumb in its mouth, but it was walking strangely.

"Ah, my little friend. I see you have the final piece of the puzzle there, which means my Malkin is complete. You don't look so good, though. Been in a fight, have you?"

The Calloskira gave him a hard look and dropped the bloody digit on the floor in front of him. The creature was covered in blood, partly from the finger but also from the wound on its side. "Ah, a fighter was she? Spirited? Well, that's interesting. Serves you right, though, taking people's fingers. Imagine!" Zed cackled, his voice echoing through the room as he knelt down. Carefully, he picked up the severed end of Jia Li's thumb and wrapped it in a small handkerchief.

"Your work is done, my good friend. Well done, and thank

you for your service. I expect you know how things go around here? We have no further use for you, so…” He paused, his grin widening. “It's time for your retirement party.”

Zed called for Olm, who came through from the bedroom, followed by three more identical quadruplets.

The Calloskira's eyes flickered with realization, but it remained still, waiting, knowing what was coming next.

“Enjoy your treat, my boys. Go get it. But do me a favour and take it outside? There's enough blood on my floor.”

The Olm brothers licked their lips. Four long black forked tongues showed themselves briefly and then slipped back inside their wide mouths. The boys converged on the wounded bat-monkey. The Calloskira shrieked.

“Very good. Very good. Now, I must finish my work. This very day, the Malkin will walk. Or perhaps tomorrow. You can't rush the master craftsman, and we want to get it right, don't we, Olm?” Zed stood up and shuffled down to his basement work-shop, leaving the group of boys to devour their victim.

As agreed, Lake met Kumiko for a morning drink in Vinod's Coffee Pot near his office. Apart from the security goons who came in with her, Lake immediately observed that Kumiko had dyed her long black hair with blue at the tips.

“Are you having a laugh?” he asked her.

“What do you mean?”

“Your hair. It's just like Rachel's, with the blue bits. Oh, never mind.”

“Sheesh, you're obsessed with that girl.” Kumiko rolled her eyes and sat down at Lake's table. Her Dream Fighter escort stayed near the door, frightening the customers inside and no doubt keeping away anyone who was thinking about coming in for a coffee.

“What made you want to see me?” Lake enquired.

Kumiko smiled sweetly. "Oh, you know. I just fancied a chat."

"What happened to: "I'm still sussing you out"? Or have you finished doing that now?"

"Oh, don't be such a drama queen. I still like you, Lakie. But this time, it's business."

"You have been busy, haven't you? Busy taking over Griffton by the look of it. Or is it the whole country? How is it that you were ready to swoop so fast? Having your own private army takes a lot of planning and preparation. Or did they just happen to be on standby, ready to save the world, just in case things started to blow up? It doesn't make sense to me."

"That's exactly why I wanted to talk to you. I want to offer you an exclusive."

"I'm listening."

"The organisation I work for is super-intelligent and very good at reading the signs."

"What do you mean?"

"They knew things were about to go pear-shaped and had already prepared a strategy to help. If you want, I can take you to our headquarters? If you like what you see, there could be a job for you with us."

"Come again?"

"Forget where you are now, the newspaper. I know for a fact they're paying you peanuts, and you're no monkey. Well, maybe a cheeky monkey."

"I like the Griffton News. My friends are there. In fact, we just got my friend back, the news editor, who was being held by those terrorists. It's a good time to be at the paper."

"No disrespect, but what I'm offering you is four times your current salary in an organisation that actually has a future. I'm talking more autonomy, and you still get your name in lights."

Lake stared at Kumiko. He liked the blue highlights in her long black hair, her flawless skin, and beautiful cat-like eyes. He liked her confidence and was attracted by her ambition.

"Kumi, you're something else."

"Tell me something I don't know." She grinned, showing a row of perfect, pearly teeth.

HER FIRST STEPS were faltering and slow, and it was with difficulty that she ascended the steps from Zed's basement. He helped her up, and soon, she was walking unaided around his pokey front room. Her stiff and mechanical movements continued, and her arms stayed at forty-five degrees for some time. Meanwhile, Zed danced around, whispering encouraging words and revelling in her every movement. Those horrible, lifelike eyes stared out from their deep sockets, dead to compassion and dead to hope. He had created a perfect monster, a perfect Malkin. She swiped at him with one hand, swinging it like a tennis racket, but Zed dodged the blow and laughed.

"Go now. Go and do what you were made to do," he commanded in a growl. The Malkin's dead eyes turned on him as she bore down on him. But his order filtered through before she reached him, and she rotated and staggered to the foot of his steps.

Zed shed a tear but clapped his hands and jumped for joy as the Malkin left his home on her long journey to the end of the earth.

He watched his baby getting smaller and smaller as her bare feet padded across the smooth black rock, her wild hair streaming behind her, and her bleak eyes locked on the horizon.

CHAPTER 22

After meeting the Rescuer, Eddie spent time exploring the vast red world, which he considered Martian. There was so much to see and experience and so many surprises. For example, he loved seeing the dark rocks that hung in the air, as light as feathers but as dense as any boulder back on Earth. He found many types of creatures that were unknown to man, as well as land configurations that stretched the imagination and the intellect.

Above all, while he walked and explored, following the directions he had been given to get back to the stone head, he enjoyed the new life that coursed through his veins. His encounter with the King banished his guilt, shame, and feelings of inadequacy forever. Under the searching glare of the Dunamis, he had decided on full disclosure, confessing his darkest thoughts and actions so that he could be operated on once and for all.

As a result, he walked this land a new man: a man renewed, with everything to live for. He knew he would never drink again. He longed to see his daughter and hold her in his arms. He loved the feeling of fellowship he now had with the Dunamis and the Creator who loved him. He despised Samyaza even more for his blackmail and deceit.

The Rescuer told him, "I am sending you back now. Live your life as best you can, clean and honest. If you stumble, you must get up again, knowing that you are a new creation, a free man. I have work for you to do in Griffton. Wait for my direction. Trust the Dunamis and follow him."

"And Rachel?"

"I have her in my gaze, but she has work of her own to do. I cannot tell you what the future holds, but stand firm, and I will provide all you need."

So, Eddie walked and sometimes danced through the valleys and over the hills, finding paths untrodden by man and enjoying the warmth of the red sun. He waded through streams and leapt over treacherous cracks that fell away to eternity, and in time he found the stone head portal. The path he had taken enabled him to avoid the house of the crazy man whose son had pushed him off the cliff. He would have liked to see that amazing black rock once again, the obsidian plateau on which the house was built.

Eddie stood and gazed at the statue. He was a tall man, but it was even taller, staring at him impassively with its deep-set eyes and waiting, just waiting. As he'd been told by the Rescuer, it was buzzing with electricity, switched on for him, and ready to go. He just hoped it would take him back home rather than to some even crazier place. Perhaps there were lands with blue or green suns you could get to through this science-fiction doorway.

He put his hand on the grey stone face, and it immediately passed through. He could feel nothing at the end of his fingertips except for air. Not wanting to leave his hand in another world, he followed it quickly with his wrist and then his upper arm. Again, it was like reaching into an open doorway. There was no resistance and certainly no impression of cold, hard stone.

"Well, in for a penny, in for a pound," he said and followed his arm into the statue. He slipped out of the mezzanine world where the sun was setting and back into Griffton in what felt like the dawn of a new day. The sun was rising, but this time, it was yellow, not the red one he'd left behind.

Griffton Cliff was empty of people, and Eddie wandered over to the edge and peered out across the city. It looked the same, but something told him things had changed down there. Scanning the city skyline, he worked out that several of the buildings were no longer there. It looked like the police station at the centre, and one of the buildings in Government Square had gone.

"Interesting," said Eddie out loud. He filled his lungs with the fresh morning air. "Good morning, Dunamis. Shall I head for my house now?"

Words formed inside him. "Yes, Eddie. It's time to go home."

"All right then. I'll go and find the car." He walked down the track that led to the lower car park on Griffton Cliff.

Driving down into Griffton, he still felt that things had changed, although he couldn't see direct evidence of this. It was something in the air. Then he saw his first smashed-up house and soon came across another. He wondered how long he had been away from home.

The next thing, he was stopped at a checkpoint outside the city centre, which was definitely something new.

The checkpoint itself was nothing more than a series of large metal petrol drums blocking the road with two men standing in the middle.

The craziest thing was that, rather than being policemen or traffic cops, the people who stopped him looked like mediaeval warriors. With the early morning sun lighting them in that stark and fresh way that it does, they looked like film extras waiting for the director to tell them what to do. They wore leather armour and sturdy helmets that covered their heads except for their faces.

Eddie wound down his window as he approached them. One of them walked round to him.

"Are you two having a laugh? Where's the camera then?"

"Where are you going to?"

"That's none of your business. Who are you, anyway?"

"Where are you going to?" asked the soldier again, hardening his tone.

"I'm going home, not that it's any of your business."

"Can I see your driver's licence?"

"No, you can't. Let me pass. Tell your friend there to stand out of the way. I don't want to run him over. If I were you, I'd pack up your stuff before the cops find out. I can see you're doing one of those outdoor battle things today, but they're not going to have a sense of humour like me."

"Have you been out of town?"

"Yeah. I've been away for a bit."

"Things have changed in the city since you've been gone," explained the Dream Fighter. "There have been some terrorist attacks. The police and the army are unable to help. We're in charge now. We're private security."

"Dressed like that?"

"Our uniform is comfortable and effective and none of your business. Now, I need to see your driver's licence."

Eddie shrugged and got his driver's licence out. If what they said was true, he was keen to check his house was in one piece.

"Okay, you can pass. But we advise you to go straight home."

"Yeah, whatever," said Eddie as he closed his window.

He didn't know about the attacks or this odd state of emergency, but he knew Rachel was safe and that his hair had turned white through his acquaintance with the Rescuer and his Dunamis. He took another look at his reflection in the sun visor that he had lowered for the purpose and chuckled.

"Distinguished. That's how you look, Ed," he said.

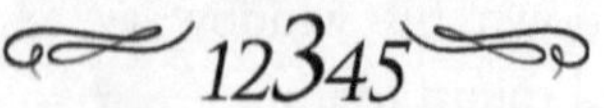

THERE WAS a smell of burning in the air as he entered Russet Road, but at least his house was intact. He had a thorough check upstairs and down, seeing nothing amiss except for the fact that Rachel wasn't home, nor had she been since she went to the other place. He was glad he'd had that time with her by the lake.

He wondered how long he'd been away, perhaps a couple of weeks. With newfound vigour, he tidied up, listening to the local radio to get up to speed on what had been happening in his city. Griffton was under attack. The country was under attack. In fact, it sounded like the whole world was under siege, living in fear of an organised and ruthless enemy that was trying to bring an end to life as they knew it. He wondered how things could flip so quickly from being relatively normal one day to being chaotic the next.

Eddie threw out his old fridge food that had gone out of date and the uneaten fruit that had gone dry. He took a whiff of the milk and poured it down the sink because it had turned. Meanwhile, he learned about the attacks on the two buildings that he had viewed from Griffton Cliff and the bus bombings and disappearances. It was all very unnerving.

In response to the civil disobedience that followed the attacks, the citizens had more or less begged a private security firm to take command in the absence of any other civic authority. So, those jokers at the checkpoint were right. These so-called Dream Fighters were now in charge, and everyone had to do what they said or else. Eddie snorted.

He left the radio on while he went to fetch his whiskey. He had three bottles on the go in different places and brought them all to the kitchen.

"Dunamis, my new friend, I'm going to need your help here." Gradually, confidence rose in him and peaked as he grabbed and opened each bottle in turn. He emptied them all down the plughole, weeping as he finished the operation. New feelings arose in him, feelings of freedom and joy, and he took his time luxuriating in these.

"Okay, Eddie. What's next?" he asked himself.

He carried his portable digital radio with him and went up to his bedroom. Piling up the plates and glasses, he took several trips down to the kitchen to deposit his loads. Next, he picked up his used clothes from the floor and dumped them in the wash basket on the landing. Dirty shirts, underwear, and trousers revealed a sea of blue carpet underneath like clouds disintegrating to show a clear sky.

On one of his trips out to the landing, he caught sight of his hair in the mirror. It was wispy and bright white, no longer brown and grey as before. Eddie grinned and carried on working. When he had finished, he sat down and wondered what he was going to do for work. He knew he had little money in the bank, and he hadn't chased work recently because he'd been so low.

"What am I going to do, Dunamis?" he asked. Almost as soon as he'd formed the thought, there was a knock at the door. Cautiously, he answered it, half expecting it to be one of those Dream Warriors coming to arrest him for thinking mutinous thoughts.

Instead, it was Corbyn from across the street. Corbyn was one of his old drinking buddies.

"Ah, Corbyn. How's tricks?"

"Hi, Eddie, I saw you were back." He had a young golden retriever on a leash, sitting at his feet. It sat obediently and licked its lips with a pink tongue.

"Yeah, I've been away."

"Out of town?"

"Yeah, you know."

"Birmingham?"

"No, somewhere else," said Eddie. He looked enquiringly at his neighbour, a man in his sixties.

"Well, sorry to bother you, but I remembered that you were

handy with plumbing and stuff. Is there any chance you could help out with a couple of jobs? I'll pay your rate, of course."

"Yes, Corbyn," laughed Eddie. "I'd be happy to. It's funny because I was just thinking about…"

"There's a couple of other neighbours who've also been asking," added Corbyn. "I don't suppose you do electrics as well? With all the problems, you know, people have had trouble, and they don't really know who to ask—or who to trust."

Eddie laughed out loud and stood tall.

"Tell them I'm the man for the job," he said confidently. "I've got all my own tools, everything I need."

One slow step after another, the Malkin walked through the rocky valley, lightning clattering and flashing in the clouds. The electrical storm in the mezzanine world generated fiery lines across the ground and, in the skies above, gold and tangerine arcs. The tiny figure picked out an unhurried path over the land and towards the stone head, which was a speck on the horizon.

The heavens seemed to take a deep breath before unleashing torrential rain that lashed down onto the floating boulders and dusty tracks. The clouds hurled their vicious arrows at the ground, soaking the parched oval valley, its scrubby under-growth, and squat bushes. At the same time, the rain found the figure of the Malkin and soaked it to the bone. Unaffected, she walked forward, her long black hair soaked and stringy, framing her hooded eyes.

A group of warrior angels had tracked her since her appear-ance in the valley, having spied her from the mountains where they stood. Flying through the clattering rain, they landed near and encircled her.

"Halt," cried the leader. He stood tall, thrusting out his chest and brandishing his sword. "I command you to halt."

His comrades stood firm and looked on with fierce eyes, each holding the hilt of his sword.

The Malkin slowed her pace even further and ground to a halt, staring at her adversaries through the curtain of her hair. Emanating great evil, she looked at them, each one, as though deciding whether or not to give herself up.

"What creature are you?" the leader demanded. Six mighty soldiers surrounded her, including the one who spoke.

She turned her head, her shoulders, and then her body to stare at him as he stood on her right-hand side.

An unearthly scream came from deep inside the Malkin. It started softly but rose to a deafening screech. All the while, her two dead eyes stared, unflinching, at their target. As the din hit its crescendo, the six warrior angels were thrown backward. They landed a great distance away, crumpled and defenceless, unable to move. The relentless rain continued to dive at them as the lightning crashed, highlighting the proud form of the Malkin.

She turned and carried on walking slowly, very slowly.

CHAPTER 23

Caleb came back laughing and joking, and the gang was overjoyed to see this. He arrived as he had left, in the arms of a massive angel who placed him gently on the ground.

"Hey, Caleb! Your hair's white like Rachel's!" Rory shouted out. Caleb grinned and put his hand to his shortly-cropped hair.

"Grey to white. Fancy that!" he said.

They embraced him as though he had been away for ages, though it had probably been less than an hour, and he kept releasing deep-throated laughs and ruffling the boys' hair. They seemed to like this and ran around him like he was some sort of funfair attraction.

Rachel was particularly encouraged by the change in him, which reassured her about recent events. He was sombre but not distraught when he spoke of Eli and Anton, and he seemed to have regained hope.

He didn't share with them what had happened to him, though, and it left them wondering whether he had visited the stars or sat amongst the angels. Mattatron, who had delivered him back to them, stood and smiled gnomically while they chatted with Caleb.

Then the angel looked serious and said, "Something urgent has just come to my attention. As you know, events are taking their course here and on Earth. We have heard that the enemy has unleashed a weapon as part of his broader plan, something he has been making for some time. It's a Malkin, fashioned in the form of a woman. We believe she is the key with which they can unlock the hidden place where Samyaza stays."

Rachel's mind boggled.

"Rachel, you have been chosen to face the Malkin alone. The Dunamis will be with you, but your friends cannot be. She will certainly destroy them."

"But what about me?"

"You are equipped to do this task. It must be you. She wears your finger and the fingers of four others."

"What?" shrieked Rachel.

"This is why it must be you."

"I don't understand."

"That is the plan. You are linked by blood to the Malkin, and you are the first of the five."

"Why can't someone else do it? What about the others?" Rachel was verging on hysteria. "I mean, how come they got my finger? Why mine? And who are the others?"

"I understand that you are linked by bloodline and share a common ancestry."

Daniel exclaimed, "Ah! I see." He nodded at Micah. "I wondered if that was the case, but I wasn't sure."

Mattatron went on, "That is all I know at this moment. As a result, you are the one. You must face the Malkin and stop her from completing her mission, but not here. This land is overrun with evil. You must face her in Griffton, your hometown. We believe that is where she is heading."

"Why Griffton, for goodness' sake? It's just a seaside city where people hang out and go surfing and stuff. It's nothing special."

"You ask, why Griffton? There is always a place where it begins. This has been the case right through human history."

"What do you mean?"

"Eden, Jerusalem, Poland, New York," said Daniel. "That's what you mean, right, Mattatron?"

"Yes. When it comes to beginnings, sometimes it's the place that you least expect, the humblest place. It's the same with people."

"So, what do I have to do?"

"You have the power to command it to stop. Everything bows to the Rescuer in the end, everything. You can command it in the name and power of the Rescuer and his Dunamis. When it comes to it, you will know. Remember your weapons."

Daniel and Arabella put their arms around Rachel, and Arabella saw she was as pale as a corpse.

"Okay, okay. So I face this Malkin and stop her getting somewhere? Where is the place, the portal thing?"

Caleb said soberly, "I've seen it. It's in Nepal, the Himalayas. I went there to see where it began, just before I met you, Daniel, and also you, Rachel. It's a place of ice and snow, and the mountains are splitting apart in preparation."

"I've seen it, too, in my dreams," sighed Rachel.

She looked at Micah, and they locked onto each other, her big brown eyes and his beautiful almond-shaped ones.

"You can do it, Rachel," he said, touching her arm.

"I've met the Rescuer and been changed by the fire of the Dunamis," Rachel declared. "He loves me, and he's with me, and that's all that matters. I can do this. I can stop this Malkin, right?"

Her group of supporters hugged and encouraged her.

"Let's go to Griffton. Let's go home," she told them.

Intrigued by her offer, Lake travelled back with Kumiko that lunchtime to Lytescote Manor, northwest of Griffton Cliff. He remembered the curving country road that led away from the city and into the countryside, but things were different out here now, with Dream Fighter checkpoints and the odd burnt-out building. Apart from that, the journey was very familiar. He was in a black stretch limo with a driver, Kumiko, and two bodyguards.

As they approached the unmistakable gates and the long driveway with its tall, fat lime trees, Lake said, "I know this place. This belongs to Daniel Harcourt, the man you got me onto with that photo, the one who had me imprisoned."

"Yeah, that's right. We took his house."

"You took it? Just like that? Isn't that stealing?"

"You were right. He was an evil man: one of those Dunamis followers. We took his house as our headquarters. It's poetic justice. It's for the common good anyway."

"So, you're telling me he's with the gang who are responsible for the bombings and the kidnappings? It makes sense."

"That's right, and bad things happen to bad people. So anyway, he's on the run now, and we've taken over. That's the way of the world."

"The way of your world, don't you mean?"

Kumiko smiled at him and touched his knee. There was a tiny pink flower on each of her long white fingernails. "If you join us, then it's the way of our world."

"I'm keeping an open mind."

They passed the long driveway and pulled up outside the house. "Do you fancy the tour?"

"You know I do."

Kumiko took Lake's hand and dragged him into the house. "You're not going to believe what we've done with this place. You've written quite a lot about our private army in your newspaper. Let me show you where they live and train. They've got this outdoor assault course in the garden out back that keeps them in shape, as well as a shooting range and one for archery. It's really neat."

"No kidding. You really enjoy this stuff, don't you?"

"I like helping people."

"So, what is it you do for this organisation?"

"I'm in charge."

Lake stared at her like she had just turned into a big pink rabbit. "You're in charge of this? Aren't you a bit…"

"Young?" she snapped.

"No, I was going to say, aren't you a bit of a psycho?"

Kumiko punched him in the arm. "Hey, news reporter. Watch your mouth."

He smiled, finding it hard to take his eyes off her. "They've got a really good gym and a snooker table, and I have an office of my own. If we start on this side of the house, we could work our way through it, and I'll show you where you could have your office."

"Sounds good to me," said Lake. "But since we're talking turkey, what is it you want me to do if I came to work for you?"

"I'll find something. To be honest, I like having you around."

"You're kidding, right?"

"Of course I am. I've got a job description in my office. It's a proper job, Lake, like I said, on four times the salary you're on now."

Lake could see she was serious, so he pulled himself back in line and embarked on the tour.

"I am keeping an open mind, Kumi, I want you to know that. Oh, and before we get too carried away, I need to get back to the office soonish. I've still got work to do."

"This way, Lake."

THE SCALE of the Elizabethan mansion was impressive, and Lake enjoyed the views from the windows across the gardens. He could see prim, well-articulated shrubs with flower beds that sat in very straight lines. An abundance of colour bloomed out there, as wooden benches presented the best views, and leafy archways hinted at further treasures that could be found in the recesses of the gardens.

"Nice place, nice place." He bumped into yet another Dream Fighter, a broad-chested monster of a man with stubble and red eyes.

"They don't say much, do they?" commented Lake.

"No, they like to stay focused. There is one thing that you do need to know, though. This is a special army, and they get their strength from somewhere else."

"They eat a good breakfast?"

"Not quite, Lake, you prune."

"So, what do you mean?"

"Why don't we go through to one of the lounges? It would be good to chat somewhere more comfortable. I'll get them to bring us a drink. What do you fancy?"

Lake glanced at her and smiled boyishly. "I meant to drink, you noodle."

"Of course, I'd be happy with a fruit juice."

They sat down in a pair of grand, gold, and pink chairs, which were surprisingly comfortable despite having hardwood armrests. The floor was covered with a thick Persian rug with an intricate powder blue, navy, and pink design. Ancient tomes with gold and green spines lined the bookshelf, and the room smelt of nuts and dust and an unusual spice that Lake couldn't identify with certainty.

"Here's the thing. It's plain to everyone that we are in a war, right?"

"Yup. We've agreed on that."

"These Dunamis followers are trying to destroy everything that we hold dear, our very civilisation and way of—"

"You can stop with the speech. I heard you on TV." Lake said, cutting her off. Kumi paused, her words faltering. Instead of continuing, she fixed him with a steady, piercing gaze.

He added, "The problem is I met one of these Dunamis followers last year. They're not that scary. The one I met seemed quite nice, in fact. He even rescued me when I was taken prisoner, and it wasn't the Dunamis people who had me. It was the other guys, the ones who blew up the hotel, remember?"

"They might seem harmless, but don't be an idiot. You've seen what they can do. You've seen the buildings they blew up and the remains of those buses."

Lake ignored her, saying, "I mean, he didn't seem like the sort, and when he introduced me to what he said was the Dunamis, it just felt really peaceful, like I'd encountered something good for the very first time. Not anything harmful."

"They are certainly very deceitful, I can tell you," nodded Kumiko.

Lake rubbed his eyes and sipped his cold orange juice. It had ice and bits of orange in it, which he liked. He raised the glass to her and asked, "Freshly squeezed?"

She nodded.

"All right then, if the Dunamis lot are the bad guys, which side are we on?"

"The one who leads us, the one who had the brilliant idea of assembling and training an army, is called Samyaza. He is the one who is in complete control of the city now and has the best interests of the citizens at heart. He's brilliant, powerful, and he cares for us."

"This is a joke, right?" Lake collapsed back in his chair, not sure whether to laugh or be horrified.

"I know about this Samyaza. I've researched him as well. He's not okay if he's even real. There was some guy last year, probably a serial killer, who took that name and blackmailed Rachel. The guys who kidnapped me followed him, and they were bad men. As far as I could gather, they used black magic, voodoo stuff probably, and they did all these rituals which gave them their power."

Kumi was nodding slowly and smiling as he spoke. Then Lake stiffened, no longer smiling. "You're not telling me that your Dream Fighters also get their power from this Samyaza? Do they do the rituals and magic as well? Why are you mixed up with this crowd, Kumi?" Lake was ashen-faced.

"Lake, you're a big boy now. You're going to have to choose your own side in the war. The enemy is going to lose. Play it smart and join us because you're way in over your head."

"Whoa there, lady, I thought you were just offering me a job, not asking me to join the nut-job brigade." His face hardened, and he drew away from her.

Kumiko suddenly looked stern. She turned to one of the Dream Fighters who was standing just outside the door. "Hongo-yama," she barked. "Show Master Emerson something. He needs convincing."

The big Dream Fighter at the door nodded, took out his sword, and pointed it at the far window. It exploded outwards, showering the shrub bed with slivers of glass.

Lake gulped. "Are you gonna do that to me next?"

Kumiko laughed out loud. "Hongo-yama, have that window replaced. And Lake, are you ready to continue our tour? I think we've chatted enough for now, but you haven't even seen a fraction of the house. There's this massive plasma screen upstairs and a kitchen to die for."

"Do I have a choice?"

"You always have a choice," said Kumiko sweetly, taking his hand. "But I don't like it when people say no to me."

CHAPTER 24

The Malkin entered Griffton at twenty past ten on a Tuesday morning, stepping through the doorway between the worlds.

She paused momentarily in front of the stone head to get her bearings and saw through the haze of her coal-black eyes she was standing high above a city. She detected that the sea was at the end, with her destination far beyond, further than she could see.

The sun above the cliff fell on her expressionless face and glinted off her rain-soaked hair. She noticed the path to her right and moved towards it, unaware that her feet were cut and bleeding from the rocky valley.

Meanwhile, down in the city, people were at their desks trying to get things done in the wake of the bombings.

Others wandered around the shops, anxiously surveying the damage, as homeworkers and homemakers checked social media for news. In the schools around Griffton, the children sat in classes, trying to concentrate.

All the while, a constant blanket of fear settled across the people like snow. They carried a fear of being attacked, a fear of disobeying the Dream Fighters, a fear of dying, and a fear of losing family members or friends. They harboured a fear of change and a fear of poverty. It kept them in line and focused their minds on accomplishing their everyday tasks, and this worked for Griffton's new management.

Incidents of rebellion were stamped on hard by the new authority, this highly organised private army that protected them. Misdemeanours were widely publicised, and the populace tacitly agreed they would toe the line for the common good. Nobody had a clue that things were about to go up a level.

MATTATRON TOOK RACHEL, the Harcourts, Micah, and Caleb through a series of caves and lit the way with a fiery torch. The children shone their flashlights at the walls and each other, safe now they were with this glowing fighter from another world.

Preparing herself for the task ahead, Rachel stayed quiet and kept her questions and worries to herself. She tried to calm her mind and enjoy the presence of the Dunamis. This was achievable with the angel in view, as well as Caleb, Daniel, and Arabella, all of whom she admired.

By using the maze of caves, which sometimes descended and sometimes ascended, they covered a lot of ground quickly. Some of the caves had an animal or metallic stench, the children observed vocally, and some had pools of liquid while others were bare. They also saw intricate patterns on the ceilings of a few of the chambers, while several of them had branch-like stone constructions that sat in their path.

Unexpectedly, the travellers popped out of a cave and into the light. They were at the end of a broad vale, an area of rocks and crevices.

It was drizzling, the first time any of them had experienced rain in this world.

"The Malkin has entered your world. We must hurry," Mattatron informed them.

At first, a few dozen drops of water sprinkled down from the sky, offering a refreshing break after their time in the caves. But by the time they reached the stone head, their clothes were soaked, heavy with rain. Lightning cracked above them, each flash followed by deep, rolling thunder, and plum-colored clouds loomed ominously overhead, thick and swollen with the promise of more rain. The air buzzed with tension as the storm grew fiercer.

Rachel could feel a biting wind cutting into her skin, and she remembered when she first entered this valley. She had faced a similar blasting wind that was cold and fierce, though her senses had malfunctioned at the time, and she wasn't sure whether she had really experienced it.

Then she saw the stone head, smoke-grey, and stern, a sentinel waiting for their return with endless patience. At first, it looked surprisingly small, a standing stone in the middle of a vast plain that lay at the mercy of the storm. They crossed the distance, and as they approached, Rachel realised it was thick and tall and able to withstand the most extreme weather.

Nothing could shift this mammoth rock. It was her marker in this beautiful but sinister land of deathly chasms, purple skies, and floating stones.

During her stay, she had been drugged with tea, plummeted off a cliff and survived the fall, and been attacked by a demon but saved by an angel. It was the land of Rachel's Pool, a place where she had tamed a leopard and encountered the Rescuer who had changed her life and left her with his Dunamis. She wondered whether she would ever return to this strange dream world again that had become such a large part of her.

"Do you think I'll ever come back here?" she asked Caleb, who was walking beside her.

"Ask the Dunamis, Rachel. See if he gives you a firm yes or no in your spirit. That's the way to cultivate hearing his voice."

As she asked her question, the answer formed inside her: "Yes," but that was all.

They reached the stone head, and the angel said, "This is

where I must leave you. I am not authorised to go with you. You will find the Malkin through there."

Rachel looked at Mattatron with alarm. The rain had died down, but the wind still whipped at his tunic and gently blow-dried his long white hair. "But I thought you were coming with us. How can I do this without you?"

"This is your battle, Rachel. Be courageous. Remember your weapons."

"I'll try my best, plus these guys will be with me."

"Yes, except for Caleb Noble."

"Caleb? You're keeping Caleb behind? But I need him!"

"This is not his mission. Caleb and I must talk further." Caleb nodded and stepped back obediently from the stone head. He was used to last-minute changes in plans and eleventh-hour instructions, such as the way of the Rescuer.

Suddenly, everyone was hugging Caleb and saying their goodbyes while Mattatron waited patiently.

"I feel like we've spent so little time together," said Daniel. "We've been reunited only to be parted."

"Yes, it has been brief, but hopefully, we'll get together again. In fact, I'm sure we will."

"Yes, so am I," Daniel answered, adding, "I am sorry for your loss, your friends Eli and Anton, I mean."

Caleb looked down. "Thank you, but they are in a better place." They finished saying their parting words, and Mattatron said to Rachel, "You are fully equipped, Rachel, so be strong."

To the group, he added, "Now go, all of you. Be alert, be careful, and the Dunamis be with you."

"I'll go through first to check it's clear," offered Daniel. "Leave it a minute or two, then come after me, Bella." He gave his wife a lingering hug and strode forward into the portal without looking back.

Daniel disappeared into the broad, stony face, and everyone waited silently. The hairs on the back of Rachel's neck bristled. Daniel didn't return.

"Okay, then. Here we go again," said Rachel, readying herself for the transition.

BELOW GROUND AT LYTESCOTE MANOR, the Dream Fighters chanted. "*Sor-cah-yah. Hom-kii-ta-ray. Who-par-key. Yor-way-mah.*"

Their days of devotion had paid off. The sceptics were now standing shoulder to shoulder with the faithful. These included the new recruits from Griffton and those who had drifted into their group through circumstance but had yet to have their first taste of Samyaza. He didn't disappoint them.

Three hundred voices joined as the crowd stood in one of the larger storage rooms, crammed together like polystyrene packing peanuts in a cardboard box. Cans, jars, and bags of flour lined the metal shelves, providing the only audience for this spectacle. The chamber smelt of sweet incense, masking the stench of bad breath, body odour, and unwashed clothing.

Over their uniforms, the men wore dark cloaks that reached the ground, only one of which was permitted to have intricate shapes and symbols embroidered across the fabric; the others were plain.

The man who wore the special garment stared at his brethren through dilated pupils. His sharp, yellow teeth flashed as he chanted, moving up and down mechanically in his mouth. "*Malkin-sah, sor-cah-yah, orr-kell-tah, Sam-yaz-eh,*" he said in a low but loud voice. He clutched a solitary candle holder with a pathetic flame that was barely alive.

Hanging over them was a stifling back mist, the mist of the presence of Samyaza, that showered them every so often with tiny sparkling stars. It was all they needed to continue their chanting with more vigour than before.

"He has come. He is with us. Samyaza will prevail," growled the leader.

IT WAS daytime on the far side of the doorway, and the sky was blue and clear. Rachel filled herself up with Griffton air and scanned the cityscape as she'd done a thousand times before. She immediately noticed the damage, the burned-out buildings, and a trail of smoke that rose from near the cliff and led down toward the town.

"What are the chances we'll find this Malkin if we follow the smoke?" Micah asked.

"There's no smoke without fire," answered Daniel. Then he added, "We'll come down with you Rachel, but it sounds like we need to stand back when it comes to whatever you have to do. The angel has faith in you, and so do we."

Rachel nodded, and they walked down the long and winding road to Lower Ledge Crossing, which led to the city.

As they walked further, they realised why they had seen smoke from the top of the cliff: it was the bushes. They were charred and gave off a smoky haze.

Cameron and Rory blew on the smoke to see if they could reignite the fire. "Don't touch, boys. It might still be hot," said Daniel.

The group of six kept walking.

The roads were relatively empty into the city, which was a surprise. Every so often, they saw big oil cans on either side of the road, which was a new thing. They didn't block the traffic route, but Daniel noted them and made a comment about why anyone would leave such big drums in the middle of nowhere.

They were forced to walk along the main road for much of the distance, as there were no pavements. When they went into single file, Daniel and Arabella led the way, followed by Micah and then the boys, with Rachel at the rear. As there were so few cars passing, they travelled along the main road easily, though the going was slow because of the children.

Several times, the boys wanted to sit down at the side of the road, and this made the journey longer and tenser than it might have been.

They walked past several houses that looked like they'd been broken into, and when they saw people, they just stared at the group without calling out a good morning. Rachel wondered if they thought she was completely mad, and maybe she was.

Eventually, they started to see more signs of life on the outskirts of the city. The flow of cars was back to a reasonable level, albeit reminiscent of Sunday morning traffic.

"It's really quiet in the city," Rachel observed.

"Still no sign of this creature," said Micah. "Do you think we'll recognise it when we see it?"

"I don't know," said Rachel. She was now walking next to Arabella, who put her arm around her and gave her a little squeeze.

At the place where Roasting Vale Lane runs parallel to the city centre, they saw their first person on fire. The woman ran screaming across their path, her hair and clothes ablaze. Arabella gasped, and they immediately stopped in their tracks. Daniel rushed after her to help her, but she sprinted down the road and disappeared out of sight.

They looked at the faces of the people who were standing and watching, but all they could see was indifference. It was as though the people of Griffton couldn't cope with what had just happened.

At the place where Roasting Vale met Stony Bridge, they met the first few people who had lost their minds. This sent the children searching for a parental hand to hold.

Agitated, drooling, and wild-eyed, these people could not be reached by conversation despite Rachel and the Harcourt family trying to connect with them.

Some people lay motionless on the pavement, their bodies still and pale, as though life had left them. Arabella knelt beside a young girl and a boy, no older than teenagers, and gently tried to rouse them. She shook their shoulders and called out softly, but neither of them stirred. Their faces were eerily calm, their eyes closed, as if peacefully asleep—but they didn't move. Arabella glanced back at the others, her face pale, a deep unease settling over the group.

Again, the people in the shops, cafes, and restaurants seemed unable or unwilling to intervene. There was a distinct lack of compassion or even interest in what was going on that Rachel found hard to comprehend. These were her people, Griffton people, whom she had grown up with. Yet they were so isolated and unwilling to reach out to each other.

At the Pomeroy Avenue intersection, two more people ran past them, on fire. Visible flames climbed up their clothes, and one of them rolled on the floor and extinguished them.

He yelled, "Don't go over there. She's down the road. She sets things on fire."

Daniel turned to Micah and said joylessly, "I think we've tracked down our Malkin."

They carried on down Roasting Vale Lane, past Broad Path, Driftwood, and Deadwood, which meant they were now near the beach.

As the road opened up, they could see the water in the distance, a wide, flat rectangle of aquamarine flecked with white foam under a cerulean blue sky. The breeze blew the taste of sea salt into Rachel's mouth, and she heard the seagulls shriek. Perhaps they had been shrieking all the time, and she had only just noticed. It felt inevitable when she saw the figure of the Malkin walking down towards the beach, leaving chaos and destruction in her wake.

Some people ran screaming, some sat and wept, others were on fire, and many lay dead.

It was the figure of a woman around her height, with black streaming hair and something odd about her arms and her movements. She seemed unhurried, walking slowly as would a holidaymaker who was exploring Griffton's long stretch of water.

After all, people travelled miles to come here, and the beach was so clean and inviting.

Rachel stared ahead but spoke firmly to the others. "I don't think you need to come any further. Keep your kids safe. I'm okay from here. I've seen things these people haven't. I've survived things from their worst nightmares. I'm Rachel Race, and I have the Dunamis in me."

Arabella touched one of her arms and Micah the other. They held her for several lingering moments with their eyes closed, and then they let her go.

CHAPTER 25

Kumiko went down to stand with her men, a lone female amongst the three hundred. She put up with their odour because she enjoyed being their prophetess and speaking for Samyaza. She also enjoyed seeing the theatrical cloud he laid on for his followers. She found the sparkling lights pretty.

She stood next to their leader in the embroidered cloak and signalled for them to stop chanting. The clouds stayed with them as she spoke on behalf of their master.

"Samyaza is satisfied with your devotion. As we speak, he is preparing to come into the world and will stand with us one day soon.

"I can also tell you we have dealt a significant blow to our enemies, and our plans continue unopposed. All across the world, we are gaining supporters by the day—in Europe, America, Africa, and the East. But there is still work to be done. We must continue, people. We *must* continue the good work. We will not rest by day or night. We will not stop, nor will we be defeated. Samyaza is King, Samyaza is Lord, Samyaza will prevail."

The crowded storeroom packed with Dream Fighters erupted in wild applause. Kumi bowed and left the place.

Around noon, she got a call from Lake Emerson. "I'm hearing crazy stuff out there. It seems like the world's gone mad. I'm hearing about people setting each other on fire and stuff. Kumi, I'm scared. What can you tell me?" he said rapidly.

"What do you mean, exactly?"

"I was hoping you could tell me what's going on today. Is it some sort of weapon? Are we talking about suicide bombers? There's people on fire and people dead."

"Is that what you're hearing, Lake? Do you remember what I told you about choosing sides? Well, now's the time. Come and join me."

"So, you know what's going on?"

"Of course I do, Lake. Come and work with me and I can tell you everything. I'll give you everything I have." She licked her lips and waited.

"Can you guys protect me? Can you keep me safe? Me and my family?" he jabbered.

"Of course we can. Come and work with us. You've seen the terms, the salary, the scope. I know you like what you saw. You don't have much of a poker face. The best thing about the job is you'll have all the info you need, and people like us love information, right? Together, we can tell the people and help them be safe. Forewarned is forearmed, right? And you're a great communicator. You'll be in a position to help people in these tough days ahead because more bad stuff is coming. Things are going to get worse, Lake. No one at the Griffton News can help you like I can." She looked at her nails and waited.

"Okay, okay. I'm in."

"That's great news, Lake. Glad to have you on board. Resign today, and I'll send you a car tomorrow. I'll have your office prepared."

"Can you tell me anything now about the new weapon?"

"Don't worry. You're safe for now. Quit, pack up, go home, and I'll see you tomorrow." Kumi ended the call.

MATTATRON TOOK Caleb up to a high hill in another part of the land, a lush valley crammed with purple and green shrubs and trees. An army of a thousand angels waited on a high ridge, some on horses and others on foot. This valley was far greater than the one Caleb had seen earlier, the one with the stone head.

Lower down in the basin were an equal number of dark creatures, monsters from Caleb's nightmares, shuffling and waiting impatiently for battle.

"What does this mean?"

"It means we need Rachel to succeed."

"And if not?"

"We need her to succeed. If not, well, the Creator knows. We are ready to fight for the sake of humanity. It helps us to partner with you, but the world is a faithless place in this current age. Few live with the Dunamis in their lives. But still, we fight for you because the Rescuer loves you, and you are precious to him."

Caleb marvelled at the glorious troops in front of him, standing tall under a maroon sky.

"There are more of us than this, many more," said Mattatron.

"It's such an honour. You are all so beautiful to behold."

"And so are you, Caleb, you and your kind. You are made in the Creator's image, and that's what makes you beautiful."

Caleb grinned. "So, now what?"

Mattatron replied, "We wait."

Rachel walked up to the Malkin, who was trudging resolutely towards the water's edge with bare feet. She saw the figure had thick, dark, wavy hair that fell down her back and was badly in need of brushing. She wore a white dress that was flapping in the breeze around her brown legs. She only had one hand, her left hand. The other arm ended in a rounded stump.

"Stop. I command you to stop," said Rachel, finding her voice. Since meeting the Rescuer, a newfound confidence had settled inside her, and made a home.

She saw the waves slide in and out, hissing and shushing. There was nobody in the sea despite it being a warm summer's day. She could see a couple of boats on the horizon and a red buoy a little nearer to shore.

The Malkin halted and turned around. "Is that you, Rachel, my child?" she said in her mother, Maryam's voice, startling her. A terrible evil emanated from her, bathing Rachel in waves of darkness.

Rachel stared at the face of her dead mother, lost for words. It had been eight years since she had last set eyes on her when she was just nine years old. It was the day her mother died in the kitchen.

"Amme?" Rachel asked at last, entranced by her mother's countenance, her huge eyes, those lips, and the brow, all of which belonged to her dear mother. Everything was as she remembered, except the eyes were different from her mother's. They were dull, drugged, and dead.

She was suddenly aware of a figure calling out from the beach road, Griffton Boulevard, where her friends stood. She tore her eyes away from her mother and saw her father running downhill. The big man bounded towards her with huge strides.

"It's not your mother, Rachel," he shouted. "Listen to me! That thing is not your mother. Don't talk—don't listen to it." She noticed that his hair was bright white, just like hers. The sunlight made it shine.

"Dad!"

"Do what you were sent to do, and do not engage with it."

Rachel remembered immediately that her weapons were joyful laughter and faith. She laughed in the creature's face with everything she had in her. She would laugh and disarm it just as she had the demon and the leopard. But as she looked back at the face of her mother, she began to cry.

She didn't know if it was the shock or the horror or the disappointment at such a cruel trick, but she cried instead of laughing, and it was all she had the strength to do. She couldn't do it: she couldn't defeat the Malkin. It felt more than she could bear.

Instead, the Malkin looked at her through her dead eyes and put her hand up to Rachel's face to stroke her. Rachel saw, for the first time, that the fingers of her left hand were all different shades, and they were sewn on. Two were light brown, one was dark brown, and two were pale. One of those fingers, the little finger, was hers. She recoiled, but the Malkin placed her hand on her cheek, her five fingers burning their impression on her face. The pain made her fall back.

Instead of Rachel, it was the Malkin who laughed. She emitted a deep and mocking laugh through the mask of a dead face, someone's twisted imitation of her mother. Her father was right: this was not Maryam.

The Malkin's laughter was a knife wound to Rachel's heart to match the searing pain in her face. She crumpled to the ground, crying with helplessness and agony.

Eddie shouted wordlessly and charged at the Malkin like a rugby player, head down, shoulders braced. His large frame collided with her side, the force of a man striking a woman who was a head shorter than him. But to his shock, the Malkin was far denser than he could have imagined. She stood unmoving, like a solid column, and Eddie rebounded off her hard body, crashing to the ground.

As he lay on the beach, winded and staring up at the Malkin, a wave of hopelessness washed over him. She seemed invincible.

Still, he prepared himself to charge again, refusing to give up—but something stopped him. A force, deep and unseen, held him back, whispering that brute strength alone would not defeat this creature.

There was a sharp screech in the air above, and a colossal creature swooped down and collected the Malkin from the beach. It was a huge, brown-winged beast, long and robust-looking, with a reptilian face and pointed wings. It seemed to come from nowhere, diving to pluck its passenger up as a seagull might descend to grab its lunch before taking off again.

Forced to stay on the ground by the wind created by its massive wings, Rachel and Eddie clutched each other and stared.

The flying creature took off with the Malkin at great speed across the English Channel, travelling in a straight line southwards and climbing higher as it went.

"I couldn't do it," Rachel wept. "I couldn't stop it. She looked so real."

"Hush, my child," said her dad, with his big muscular arms around her. "I'm sure there'll be another way. There has to be another way." He sat and stared across the water, holding his daughter tightly, tears in his eyes.

Soon, Daniel, Arabella, Micah, and the kids encircled them and were consoling Rachel and seeking the Dunamis to make some sense of the situation.

12345

AFTER DEPARTING BRITISH SHORES, they flew directly over France, that mighty republic that the Dream Fighters now controlled from their Paris base, from La Havre to Marseille, La Rochelle to Strasbourg.

Soon, Barcelona lay beneath them, where the people continued to riot and loot in the wake of their broken economy.

They entered the airspace above Algeria and Libya, which faced food shortages and civil unrest. Several pilots had to double-check that they really had seen a gigantic, flying reptile clutching a woman in its talons.

Egypt was next, that ancient land where the people were now at each other's throats, grabbing what they could for themselves. East towards Saudi and Iran, they went where the rulers had been overthrown, and the nations were in flux, about to be reordered under the Dream Fighters' strong leadership. Oil fields became battlegrounds, and food and water prices soared into the sky like the winged creature above their heads.

The long wastelands of southern Afghanistan gave way to the dry mountains of north-eastern Pakistan and India. In time, the winged worm came to Nepal, the end of its journey, with its snowy peaks and treacherous heights.

CHAPTER 26

The snow had come overnight and coated the mountain ridges ahead, but the beauty of the scene was lost on the winged creature and its passenger. They flew over Tumlingtar, confusing the pilots who were just leaving the runway on their way to Kathmandu.

They passed through Makalu-Barun, the Himalayan glacier valley at the base of Mount Makalu. Beneath them was a dome-shaped cave, five hundred feet high, with a long waterfall coming out of its stone roof.

They showed no interest in the stunning waterfall that cascaded from high down into the depths of the deep gorges or the craggy rocks that rose from lush green forests, where colourful flowers bloomed beneath snow-white peaks.

Regardless, they flew on, heading for the mountain itself, aiming for Makalu on the border of Tibet and Nepal, which was now roaring in anticipation. The mountain, which rose to almost eight and a half thousand feet, had a long crack at its base but still held firm, unable to eject its prisoners until the portal was unlocked.

The flying creature descended rapidly and dumped the Malkin within walking distance of the mountain wall. It retreated to a plateau and sat down to rest, having accomplished the journey from the Griffton stone head without stopping.

Pale from the icy winds, the Malkin trod the icy path to the base of the mountain. A vertical wall that sat beneath the distinctive pyramidal peak with its four faces.

Staring into space, the Malkin placed her hand against the mountain, finding the five-fingered indentation next to the crack. It exactly matched the five fingers on her left hand. She touched each one in turn to their corresponding impressions, first Rachel's, then José's, Ndege's middle finger, Paulo's, and finally Jia Li's thumb.

There was a slow crunching sound, a low booming, and the crashing echo of an avalanche as the mountain opened.

RACHEL and the gang had all returned to her house. Her dad made coffee for everyone and soft drinks for the children. She was enjoying having people in the house again despite the circumstances. Unexpectedly, though, Rachel felt intense pain in her left hand that centred on the stump of her missing finger.

It was the first time in ages that her finger had hurt her so much. It made her yelp with pain, and her father looked concerned and asked if she was all right.

"I'm all right, but it hasn't done this for ages. Not since it healed up last year. I mean, sometimes it hurts if I knock it, but never this sharp pain. Maybe it's a nerve ending, you know, complaining."

"No. It's no coincidence. This doesn't bode well," said Daniel, voicing what everyone was thinking.

For José, on his father's farm in Bolivia, it was his fourth finger that suddenly caused him pain. For Paulo, Ndege, and Jia Li, it was their respective fingers, or thumb in the case of Jia Li, who let out a sharp cry, causing her comrades to stare at her. They had been alarmed by the attack of the winged creature, well aware of the stories of strange monsters that dwell in the high mountains. Jia Li's friend, Jing Yi, checked her stump and put her hand on her shoulder, feeling helpless that there was nothing she could do. Jia Li nodded in thanks, her eyes wet with tears. She patted Jing Yi's hand.

BOTH THE MALKIN and the winged creature were incinerated by the fire that belched out from the mouth of the portal. Nothing was left of them. A large quantity of snow was also blasted by the flames and turned into liquid that poured down the slopes, clearing the way for the coming Grigori.

The sound of stamping could be heard, not that there was anyone nearby to hear it. Stamping, growling, and roaring filled the mountain air, at first sounding like it was coming from far down in the mountain's core. Feral noises echoed around inside and were ejected by the gaping slit in the mountain.

The sounds grew louder, starting as a noisy rumbling in Mount Makalu's stomach that increased steadily in volume until it became a thunderous roar. The mountain was gearing up to vomit the Watchers and their Nephilim out onto the Earth.

Then it happened, the emergence of the ancient ones, the Watchers, an ancient evil that had been locked beneath the mountains and the valleys. They had waited for centuries, millennia, in fact. Today was their day, the day of the Grigori.

With slow, prehistoric steps and dull eyes, Samyaza, the leader of the rebellion, stepped out of the portal, free at last.

Once an angel of light, now darkened by pride and hatred, he stepped into the world once more. His hideous face contorted with rage. He spread his wings, threw back his head, and roared at the sky. The disturbance could be heard across the mountain region that covered Nepal, Tibet, China, India, Pakistan, and Bhutan.

Behind him, the rest of the two hundred Grigori shoved

each other impatiently to get to the surface with their beautiful, horrific offspring, the Nephilim, at their heels.

Today was the day the world changed.

RACHEL SAT bolt upright and turned to her companions, who had gathered around her as she sat on the sofa.

"I need to find the others. I'm going back to the stone head. I need to be with the others. We have to stop Samyaza."

"Slow down, Rach. What others?" asked her father.

"The ones who lost their fingers. I can reach them through the stone head. I'm sure of it. You can come with me if you want, but I need to go. I need to go right now."

ACKNOWLEDGMENTS

A big thank you to my editors, Phoebe, Dan, Clare, Rob, and Natalie, and my friends at The Book Whisperer, Anya especially. And to my growing band of supporters and readers at home and abroad – an ocean-sized thank you!

Thanks also for inspiration and a solid soundscape to Brian 'Head' Welch, Love & Death, Foo Fighters, Soundgarden, We Are Jonah, Kim Walker-Smith, Living Sacrifice, Metallica, Alice in Chains, Faith No More, Megadeth, Led Zeppelin, Queens of the Stone Age and Candlemass. You guys all totally rock, and you know it.

ABOUT THE AUTHOR

Joshua Raven has enjoyed thirty years as an international journalist, editor, business copywriter and media consultant. As a novelist he has been a featured author at the Dubai Emirates Airline Festival of Literature. And as a journalist and professional writer he has interviewed leading figures in business and technology, including Bill Gates and Michael Dell, and written for publications and businesses across the globe including The Times newspaper, Microsoft, Google and Facebook. Joshua lives in the South of England and enjoys people, music, cooking, reading, and travelling.

facebook.com/JoshuaRavenAuthor

x.com/RavenWrites

instagram.com/RavenWrites

linkedin.com/in/arif-mohamed-71b2831a

amazon.com/stores/Joshua-Raven/author/B0034O22RS

pinterest.com/joshuaraven75

ALSO BY JOSHUA RAVEN